U0105960

英语专业四级

听力指南（第二版）

A Guide to the Listening Comprehension in TEM 4

常春藤英语考试研究组　编　著

上海交通大学出版社

内 容 提 要

　　本书是根据《高校英语专业四级考试大纲》(2004 年新版),专门为参加英语专业四级考试的考生编写的一本听力考试应试书。书中讲解了四级听力考试应试技巧,选编了 10 套听力模拟题。所选材料新颖,针对性强,可使广大考生在短期内提高听力水平和应试能力。

图书在版编目（C I P）数据

　　英语专业四级听力指南 / 常春藤英语考试研究组著.
2 版. —上海:上海交通大学出版社,2006（2007 重印）
　ISBN 978 - 7 - 313 - 03798 - 5

　　Ⅰ. 英... Ⅱ. 常... Ⅲ. 英语—听说教学—高等学校—水平考试—自学参考资料　Ⅳ. H319.9

　　中国版本图书馆 CIP 数据核字（2004）第 063859 号

英语专业四级听力指南
（第 2 版）
常春藤英语考试研究组　编著
上海交通大学出版社出版发行
（上海市番禺路 877 号　邮政编码 200030）
电话:64071208　出版人:韩建民
上海颛辉印刷厂印刷　　全国新华书店经销
开本:880mm×1230mm　1/32　印张:6.5　字数:181 千字
2004 年 8 月第 1 版　2006 年 7 月第 2 版　2007 年 3 月第 5 次印刷
印数:23151 - 28200
ISBN 978 - 7 - 313 - 03798 - 5/H·760　定价（含 MP3）:20.00 元
ISBN 978 - 7 - 88844 - 238 - 2

前　　言

　　《英语专业四级听力指南》是根据《高等学校英语专业基础阶段教学大纲》和《高校英语专业四级考试大纲》(2004 年新版)编写的听力应试辅导书。本书的试题严格按照新编考试大纲编写，并参照了 2005 年考试真题，使本书较之第一版内容更新，在难易度上更接近真题。

　　本书第一部分是应试指导，分听写和听力理解两部分。每部分对新考试大纲和应试技巧都作了说明，旨在使考生理解考试的目的、方法和技巧，从而具有明确的考试目标和手段。本书第二部分是 10 套仿真试题，使考生得到充分的考前训练，通过训练，考生对考试具有很强的感性认识和应试能力，考生可以学到丰富的语言和背景知识，在未来的考试中能够应付自如。

　　本书试题形式与真题完全一致，考生应该模拟真实的考试场景，按照要求在规定时间内完成每套试题。然后用更多的时间来精听，做到基本上理解所听的内容，学到新的语言和背景知识。

　　本书由朱篱执笔。

常春藤英语考试研究组

2006 年 4 月

目　录

第一部分　英语专业四级听力应试指导·················· 1

听写 ··· 1

听力理解 ····································· 4

第二部分　英语专业四级听力模拟题 ·············· 10

PRACTICE TEST　1 ························· 10

PRACTICE TEST　2 ························· 18

PRACTICE TEST　3 ························· 26

PRACTICE TEST　4 ························· 34

PRACTICE TEST　5 ························· 42

PRACTICE TEST　6 ························· 50

PRACTICE TEST　7 ························· 58

PRACTICE TEST　8 ························· 66

PRACTICE TEST　9 ························· 74

PRACTICE TEST 10 ························· 82

第三部分　英语专业四级听力文字材料 ·········· 90

TAPESCRIPT OF PRACTICE TEST　1 ········· 90

TAPESCRIPT OF PRACTICE TEST　2 ········· 101

TAPESCRIPT OF PRACTICE TEST　3 ········· 112

TAPESCRIPT OF PRACTICE TEST　4 ········· 123

TAPESCRIPT OF PRACTICE TEST　5 ········· 133

TAPESCRIPT OF PRACTICE TEST　6 ········· 143

TAPESCRIPT OF PRACTICE TEST 7 ···················· 154
TAPESCRIPT OF PRACTICE TEST 8 ···················· 165
TAPESCRIPT OF PRACTICE TEST 9 ···················· 176
TAPESCRIPT OF PRACTICE TEST 10 ···················· 187

第四部分　答案··· 198

第一部分　英语专业四级听力应试指导

听写

一、考试大纲

2004 年新版《高校英语专业四级考试大纲》(以下简称《大纲》)对四级听写作了如下的规定：

1. 测试要求

(1) 能在全面理解内容的基础上逐字逐句写出所听材料。

(2) 拼写和标点符号正确无误,错误率不超过 8%。

(3) 考试时间 15 分钟。

2. 测试形式

本部分为主观试题。所听材料共听四遍。第一遍用正常速度朗读,录音语速为每分钟 120 个单词,让学生听懂材料大意。第二、三遍朗读时意群、分句和句子之间留出约 15 秒的空隙,让学生书写。第四遍再用正常速度朗读,让学生检查。

3. 测试目的

测试学生听力理解能力、拼写熟练程度以及正确运用标点符号的能力。

4. 选材原则

(1) 题材广泛,体裁多样。

（2）听写材料难度不超过《高等学校英语专业教学大纲》规定为准。

（3）听写材料长度约 150 个单词。

二、应试技巧

1. 理解全文内容

在听第一遍录音时，考生要集中精力听懂文章的主要内容，抓住中心大意，理解文章的篇章结构和上下文逻辑关系，不要急于书写，否则会抓不住重点。只有在听懂文章主题以后，才能够启动理解某一主题所需要的语言和非语言性知识，准确理解文章的内容，为准确书写做好准备。

2. 按意群书写

听写文章总分成若干个意群，每个意群可能是词组、分句或单句。在第二遍朗读录音时，要以意群为单位去理解。在听意群时要抓关键句型和关键词，在听第三遍时，再把其他次要的内容补上。一些来不及写的词可用缩略形式或符号代替，等最后一遍或最后复查两分钟时写出完整的词。听写的评分主要是看能否写出文章的主要信息，然后再对一些小的错误扣分。总之，要按意群来听写，因为听写成绩是以 15 个意群分割成 15 分，每个意群一分，所以个别词或句子的错误或遗漏不会影响其他意群的得分。

3. 把握标点符号

标点符号也是听写的一项内容。在读第二、三遍时，意群之间有 15 秒的间隙。在大部分情况下，每个间隙有一标点符号，但有些没有，这要求考生根据上下文语境正确理解每个句子，听出一些长句中的短语或分句。标点符号不是靠听出来的，但一些基本的标点如逗号、句号、引号、冒号要求考生能够正确的掌握。

4. 重视复查

在听完第二、三遍后，可以写出文章的主要内容，但一些细节还是会被漏掉或写错。这就需要好好利用第四遍和最后两分钟复查时间，检查书写内容中的小错，如拼写、搭配或遗漏等，使最后的文章通顺准确。

三、样题分析

下面就 2004 年新考试大纲的听写样题进行分析。

THE RAILWAYS IN BRITAIN

The success of early railways, such as the lines between big cities,／led to a great increase in railway building in Victorian times.／Between 1835 and 1865 about 25,000 kilometres of track were built,／and over 100 railway companies were created.／

Railway travel transformed people's lives.／Trains were first designed to carry goods.／However, a law in the 19th century forced railway companies to run one cheap train a day／which stopped at every station and cost only a penny a mile.／Soon working class passengers found they could afford to travel by rail.／Cheap day excursion trains became popular and seaside resorts grew rapidly.／

The railways also provided thousands of new jobs:／building carriages, running the railways and repairing the tracks.／

Railways even changed the time.／The need to run the railways on time meant that local time was abolished／and clocks showed the same time all over the country.／

这篇短文的主题是英国的铁路史，因此，与铁路相关联的概念和词汇如 lines，track，train，passengers，rail，carriages 等，就容易听出来。同时，各段落的主题句也有助于理解每段的内容。

该段划分为 15 个意群，大部分意群之间隙有标点符号，但有几点要注意：

插入语要用逗号隔开，如第一句中的 such as the lines between big cities；在总说性话语的后边，表示引起下文的分说要用冒号，如第三段中 new jobs 后面用了分号；一些过渡连接词要用逗号隔开，如第二段第二句中的 However 后使用了逗号。

听写材料中一般不会出现深奥的词汇和偏僻的专有名词，但有些常识性的东西是必须要掌握的，如第一段中的 Victorian 不应该写错。

听写材料由英美专家朗读，这会涉及到英美语读音的差异，如第一段中的 kilometre 就会因为英国英语和美国英语的差异在读音上有很大的不同。

听力理解

一、考试大纲

《大纲》有关听力理解部分作了如下的规定：

1. 测试要求

（1）能听懂英语国家人士关于日常生活和社会生活的谈话，以及中等难度（如 TOEFL 中短文）的听力材料。能理解大义，领会说话者的态度、感情和真实意图。

（2）能听懂相当于 VOA 正常速度和 BBC 新闻节目的主要内容。

（3）能辨别各种英语变体（如美国英语、英国英语、澳大利亚英语等）。

（4）考试时间约 15 分钟。

2. 测试形式

本部分采用多项选择题，分三节：Section A，Section B，和 Section C，共 30 题。

Section A：Conversations 本部分含有若干组对话，每组约 200 单

词。每组对话后有若干道题。本部分共有 10 题。

Section B：Passages 本部分含有若干篇短文，每篇长度约为 200 个单词。每篇后有若干道题。本4分共有 10 题。

Section C：News Broadcast 本部分含有若干段 VOA 或 BBC 新闻，每段新闻后有若干道题。本部分共有 10 题。

每部分每道题后有约 5 秒的间隙，要求学生从所给的四个选项中选出一个最佳答案。录音速度为每分钟约 120 个单词，念一遍。

3. 测试学生获取口头信息的能力

4. 选材原则

（1）对话和短文部分的内容与日常生活和学习生活相关。

（2）VOA 和 BBC 新闻材料为学生所熟悉的一般新闻报道、短评或讲话等。

（3）听力材料所出现的词语原则上不超出《高等学校英语专业教学大纲》规定的范围。

二、题型分析

听力理解部分的问题共有两大类，一是直接问题，包括复述题和事实细节题，二是间接问题，包括推断归纳题和态度题。这些问题既针对需要短暂记忆的信息，又针对必须经过归纳、判断、猜测或推理才能理解的内容。以下是对上述问题的进一步说明。

1. 复述题

复述题针对听力语料的某一部分的内容来提问，这包括单词、短语、句子或段落，要求对所听内容释义，而选项通常用与原文不同的词或词组表达与原文相同或相近的意思。例如 2005 年试题有这样一个问题：

The museum was built in memory of those _____.

　A. who died in wars

B. who worked to help victims

C. who lost their families in disasters

D. who fought in wars

该问题是针对录音中 It tells the story of men and women who, in the course of the major events of the last 150 years, have given assistance to victims of war and natural disasters 这句话设定的。所以只要能听懂这句话,解题就很方便了。

2. 事实和细节题

事实和细节题占很大的比例,要求考生对所听内容的事实和细节进行辨认和推敲,找出相关事实和细节,排除不相关的事实和细节。请看《大纲》样题:

John: Hello, Mark. Have you ever played cricket?

Mark: No, never. Have you, John?

John: No, but I once watched a game at the Cricket Club.

Mark: Did you enjoy it?

John: No, not much, though everybody else seemed to. I found it very slow. Nothing much seemed to happen. Perhaps that was because I didn't really understand what was going on.

Mark: It's a bit like baseball, isn't it?

John: Well, not really. In baseball there is only one man with a bat but in cricket there are two.

Mark: Both at the same time?

John: No. They take turns. They each stand at one end of the pitch in front of some sticks called "stumps" or the "wicket." A member of the other team, the "bowler," throws the ball at the stumps. The batsman tries to protect the wicket and hit the ball as far as he can.

Mark: What does the other team do?

John：One of them runs after the ball and throws it at the wicket. If he hits it while the batsmen are still running, one of them is out.

针对该段对话的问题是：

1. A batsman in cricket does all the following EXCEPT
_____.

   A. waiting for the other batsman

   B. standing in front of the wicket

   C. trying to hit the ball

   D. running to change positions

2. What does the bowler do?

   A. He runs after the ball.

   B. He changes positions.

   C. He throws the ball.

   D. He tries to hit the ball.

第一个问题要求考生将对话中的事实和细节进行辨认和推敲，以排除不相关信息，选项 A 为正确答案；第二个问题则要求考生找出相关信息，选项 C 为正确答案。

3. 推论归纳题

对所听内容进行推论或归纳是听力的一个重要技能。推论归纳题要求考生以所听到的内容为线索，借助常识和上下文的逻辑关系来推断或归纳没有直接表述的内容。例如：

BBC's weather forecast is a _____ programme.

   A. seldom watched

   B. little known

   C. new

   D. popular

该问题所针对的内容是：

In Britain, just after the main television news programmes,

audience figures rise. It's weather forecast time.

这一部分的内容是说,英国电视新闻节目之后观众人数会上升,那是因为接下来是气象预报时间。从这一内容可以推断出选项 C 是问题的答案。

4. 态度题

考试大纲要求考生领会说话者的态度、感情和真实意图,因此考生要理解说话人所表露出的态度和情绪。例如《大纲》样题中有这样一个问题:

What do Mark and John think about cricket and baseball?

A. Both prefer cricket to baseball.

B. Both prefer baseball to cricket.

C. Mark disagrees with John.

D. It is not clear from the conversation.

该问题所针对的内容是:

Mark:That sounds a little like baseball.

John:Not really. I think baseball is more exciting.

Mark:Yes, so do I.

从该段内容可以看出,谈话双方都认为棒球更刺激。所以选项 B 为正确答案。

三、应试技巧

新的考试大纲增加了题目难度,对考生听力能力提出了更高的要求。首先在测试形式上作了较大的改动。Section A 由原来的单句陈述改为三篇 200 字长短的对话;Section B 由原来的小对话改为三篇 200 字长短的短文。由此可见,新大纲所规定的听力内容篇幅大,增加了信息的密度,这对考生的理解和记忆都是一个不小的挑战。以下几点可以作为应试技巧供考生参考。

1. 注重预读

在听音前要利用间隙预读所问问题及选项内容,这样可以预测所听材料的大致内容,从而启动理解某一话题所需要的语言和背景知识,缩小听力理解的范围,减轻理解和记忆的负担;预读也可以提早知道哪些事实和细节在听音时要特别留意,哪些事实和细节可以忽略不记。

2. 全神贯注,边听边记录

在预读题目之后,就应该仔细听懂录音的内容,而不是边听边看题目,因为这样做虽然可以抓住一些细节,但失去的是对录音内容的全面把握。另外,由于所听内容信息量大,大脑不可能在短时间内记住所有信息,所以在听音的同时做一些笔记是非常有用的,如关键词、地点、时间、年代、数字等。

3. 不同体裁侧重使用不同方法

听力理解的三个部分(对话、短文、新闻)要用不同的方法。短文部分要求区分主要和次要信息,因此,听音时不但要听懂文章的主旨,还要听懂支撑主旨的细节,这就要求考生抓住主旨句以及各个段落的主题句,听懂了主旨句或段落主题句后,一些事实和细节就变得明朗起来,就更容易听懂;对话没有段落的区分,这要求考生紧跟说话者的语流和思路,要留心说话者的语音语调,把握说话者的语气和态度;新闻要求考生注重所涉及的人物、事件、地点、时间、原因等方面的信息,而新闻的主旨一般在第一句给出,它也是测试的对象。

4. 放松心情

由于听力内容只播放一遍,考生不免会产生紧张情绪。考试时如果有部分内容没有听懂,要学会放弃这些内容而将注意力集中在后面的内容上,否则就可能由于慌张而影响听懂后面的内容。因此,考生平时可多参加一些模拟考试,培养心理素质,增强考场的适应能力,要学会从整体而非逐字逐句理解听力材料,并学会放弃没有听懂的内容,这样考试时才能从容自信。

第二部分　英语专业四级听力模拟题

PRACTICE TEST 1

PART Ⅰ　DICTATION　　　　　　　　　　　[15 MIN.]

Listen to the following passage. Altogether the passage will be read to you four times. During the first reading, which will be read at normal speed, listen and try to understand the meaning. For the second and third readings, the passage will be read sentence by sentence, or phrase by phrase, with intervals of 15 seconds. The last reading will be read at normal speed again and during this time you should check your work. You will then be given 2 minutes to check through your work once more.

PART Ⅱ　LISTENING COMPREHENSION　　　[15 MIN.]

In sections A, B and C you will hear everything once only. Listen carefully and then answer the questions that follow.

SECTION A　CONVERSATIONS

In this section you will hear several conversations. Listen to the conversations carefully and then answer the questions that follow.

Questions 1 to 3 are based on the following conversation. At the end of the conversation, you will be given 15 seconds to answer the questions.

Now listen to the conversation.

10

1. The reason that Sally chose to study Chinese literature is that
   _____.
   A. her parents asked her to do so
   B. she is interested in Chinese culture
   C. she wants to be a China scholar
   D. she had majored in literature at college
2. What does Sally like most about her study?
   A. Variety of activities.　　　　B. Independent study.
   C. Emphasis on seminars.　　　　D. Discussion with professors.
3. All of the following are true of Sally's place of study EXCEPT
   _____.
   A. there is no snow
   B. it is a lonely place
   C. there is a lack of artistic environment
   D. you can get refreshed at the beach

   Questions 4 *to* 6 *are based on the following conversation. At the
end of the conversation, you will be given* 15 *seconds to answer the
questions.*
   Now listen to the conversation.

4. What is true of the 15 BASE jumpers?
   A. They hit the ground in more than eight seconds.
   B. They hit the ground in about five seconds.
   C. They opened their parachutes upon jumping.
   D. They hit the ground with some injuries.
5. BASE jumping differs from skydiving in that _____.
   A. BASE jumping involves more teamwork.
   B. skydivers don't make as many errors as BASE jumpers
   C. BASE jumping allows for fewer errors than skydiving

D. skydivers fall at a lower speed than BASE jumpers

6. What is true of BASE jumping?

    A. It is as popular as skydiving.

    B. It is not an exclusive sport.

    C. It is safer than skydiving.

    D. It lacks excitement.

Questions 7 to 10 are based on the following conversation. At the end of the conversation, you will be given 20 seconds to answer the questions.

Now listen to the conversation.

7. Relative happiness means _____.

    A. you have a lot of material goods

    B. you are as happy as others

    C. you're happier than before

    D. you are happier than others

8. What is true of the past definitions of happiness?

    A. They were based on self-gratification.

    B. They varied greatly.

    C. They were based on lifestyles.

    D. They described the fundamental nature of happiness.

9. Lisa seems to _____ the past definitions of happiness.

    A. misunderstand   B. be uncertain about

    C. disagree with   D. sympathize with

10. Unlike happiness, satisfaction _____.

    A. is easier to achieve

    B. has to do with one's overall life

    C. is less complicated

    D. is based on instant gratification

SECTION B PASSAGES

In this section, you will hear several passages. Listen to the passages carefully and then answer the questions that follow.

Questions 11 to 13 are based on the following passage. At the end of the passage, you will be given 15 seconds to answer the questions.

Now listen to the passage.

11. People in developed countries have some problem deciding _____.
    A. what to eat   B. how to eat
    C. where to eat   D. how much to eat

12. The majority of people in developing countries have all the following problems EXCEPT _____.
    A. eating food of a wrong kind
    B. eating food that lacks nutrition
    C. having barely enough food
    D. having little or nothing to eat

13. According to the World Bank report, to keep themselves healthy, people in developing countries should _____.
    A. follow the lifestyles of people in developed countries
    B. increase their ability to obtain food
    C. ration their food
    D. select their food carefully

Questions 14 to 17 are based on the following passage. At the end of the passage, you will be given 20 seconds to answer the questions.

Now listen to the passage.

13

14. Employers fail to _____.

    A. spend time and money on training

    B. spend time and money on continuing education

    C. take care of employee spirit

    D. improve workplace environment

15. According to the passage, we are not aware that _____.

    A. training can increase productivity

    B. an improved workplace setting can increase productivity

    C. our jobs affect our workplace setting

    D. our relationship with our employers is important

16. Workplace settings of different corporations are _____.

    A. old-fashioned   B. never debated

    C. different   D. universal

17. The workplace of all corporations will include _____.

    A. barrier-free offices   B. private offices

    C. cubicle settings   D. none of these

Questions 18 *to* 20 *are based on the following passage. At the end of the passage, you will be given* 15 *seconds to answer the questions.*

Now listen to the passage.

18. According to the latest discovery, humans began using fire about _____ years ago.

    A. 100,000   B. 250,000

    C. 500,000   D. 750,000

19. The newly discovered fire was used by humans because the burned wood _____.

    A. was plenty   B. was half burned

C. was here and there   D. was in clusters

20. What should European archeologists be doing now?

A. Find the earliest human settlements in Europe.

B. Study the methods early humans used to control fire.

C. Look for the earliest human use of fire in Europe.

D. Explain why humans settled in Europe.

SECTION C   NEWS BROADCAST

Questions 21 and 22 are based on the following news. At the end of the news item, you will be given 10 seconds to answer the questions.

Now listen to the news.

21. According to the World Health Organization, the outbreak of bird flu _____.

A. has been brought under control

B. has run out of control

C. could run out of control

D. has been exaggerated

22. Bird flu has caused human casualties in _____.

A. Thailand   B. Vietnam

C. Japan   D. South Korea

Questions 23 and 24 are based on the following news. At the end of the news item, you will be given 10 seconds to answer the questions.

Now listen to the news.

23. The news focuses on _____.

A. the legality of executing people under 18

B. the widespread death penalty in the US

C. the tasks of the Supreme Court

D. crimes committed by people under 18

24. The Supreme Court _____ approve the execution.

A. is likely to

B. will surely

C. is not likely to

D. cannot be determined from the news

Question 25 is based on the following news. At the end of the news item, you will be given 5 seconds to answer the question.

Now listen to the news.

25. Relief workers will be focusing on _____.

A. getting more search teams and equipment from abroad

B. caring for those who have been left homeless

C. searching for those who are still buried under the rubble

D. inspecting the quality of houses in nearby areas

Questions 26 to 28 are based on the following news. At the end of the news item, you will be given 15 seconds to answer the questions.

Now listen to the news.

26. Most poor people live in _____

A. Asia   B. Africa

C. Latin America   D. the Pacific

27. So far attention has been focused on _____.

A. poverty in Asia

B. poverty in Africa

16

C. success in some Asian countries

D. gaps between rich and poor countries

28. To manage Asia's growth in a more stable and inclusive way is to

    _____.

    A. reduce the wealth gaps

    B. give women equal rights

    C. follow the examples of booming economies

    D. make ethnic groups live in harmony

Questions 29 *and* 30 *are based on the following news. At the end of the news item, you will be given* 10 *seconds to answer the questions.*

Now listen to the news.

29. _____ of the Asian markets mentioned in the news closed higher for the week.

    A. All   B. Some

    C. One   D. None

30. The real estate stocks of which of the following markets moved higher?

    A. Hong Kong and Taiwan

    B. Taiwan and Tokyo

    C. Tokyo and South Korea

    D. Hong Kong and South Korea

PRACTICE TEST 2

PART Ⅰ DICTATION [15 MIN.]

Listen to the following passage. Altogether the passage will be read to you four times. During the first reading, which will be read at normal speed, listen and try to understand the meaning. For the second and third readings, the passage will be read sentence by sentence, or phrase by phrase, with intervals of 15 seconds. The last reading will be read at normal speed again and during this time you should check your work. You will then be given 2 minutes to check through your work once more.

PART Ⅱ LISTENING COMPREHENSION [15 MIN.]

In sections A, B and C you will hear everything once only. Listen carefully and then answer the questions that follow.

SECTION A CONVERSATIONS

In this section you will hear several conversations. Listen to the conversations carefully and then answer the questions that follow.

Questions 1 to 3 are based on the following conversation. At the end of the conversation, you will be given 15 seconds to answer the questions.

Now listen to the conversation.

1. Maradona's condition can be best described as _____.
   A. serious
   B. improving slightly
   C. nothing serious

D. cannot be determined from the conversation

2. The two speakers seem to agree on _____.
   A. Maradona as a role model
   B. Maradona's dazzling performance in 1986
   C. Maradona's damaging drug abuse
   D. Maradona as a human being

3. What is true toward the end of the conversation?
   A. The two speakers have solved their differences.
   B. One speaker is persuaded by the other.
   C. The two speaks remain divided in their opinions.
   D. The two speakers have broadened their differences.

   Questions 4 to 7 are based on the following conversation. At the end of the conversation, you will be given 20 seconds to answer the questions.

   Now listen to the conversation.

4. What conclusion can we draw about Mike before he went to the camping school?
   A. Mike was eager to do the course.
   B. Mike had done outdoor activities.
   C. Mike enjoyed life in the open.
   D. Mike was reluctant and timid.

5. According to the conversation, Mike was talking about the camping school experiences because _____.
   A. he enjoyed what he had done
   B. he still felt the horror of it
   C. persuaded people not to go
   D. he felt good about the result

6. Mike participated in all of the following activities EXCEPT

_____.

  A. hiking   B. canoeing

  C. swimming   D. camping

7. Which of the following words is most appropriate to describe Mike after the camping schools?

  A. Independent.   B. Strong.

  C. Determined.   D. Persistent.

  Questions 8 *to* 10 *are based on the following conversation. At the end of the conversation, you will be given* 15 *seconds to answer the questions.*

  Now listen to the conversation.

8. Which of the following is true of the speakers?

  A. Both speakers are objective about city and country life.

  B. One speaker is biased against country life while the other is not.

  C. Both speakers are biased against country life

  D. Both speakers are biased against city life.

9. Which of the following is NOT true of country life?

  A. The transportation is affordable.

  B. There is a measured pace of life.

  C. There is more planning.

  D. There are more restrictions.

10. What is true of the crimes in the country?

  A. There are no petty crimes.

  B. There are no murders.

  C. The crimes are often committed by strangers.

  D. Murders are caused by domestic violence.

SECTION B   PASSAGES

In this section, you will hear several passages. Listen to the passages carefully and then answer the questions that follow.

Questions 11 to 13 are based on the following passage. At the end of the passage, you will be given 15 seconds to answer the questions.

Now listen to the passage.

11. The number of acres of virgin forests that existed in Washington and Oregon before the 1800's is _____.
    A. 6 million   B. 60 million
    C. 600 million   D. none of these

12. According to conservationists, old growth is valuable because _____.
    A. it creates beautiful scenery
    B. it promotes the growth of other trees
    C. it purifies water
    D. promotes local economy

13. Which statement is true?
    A. The national government cares little about old growth.
    B. The local authorities discourage the cutting down of old growth.
    C. Only younger trees have been cut down in recent years.
    D. The harvesting of old growth is not likely to stop any time soon.

Questions 14 to 17 are based on the following passage. At the end of the passage, you will be given 20 seconds to answer the questions.

Now listen to the passage.

14. Running differs from other kinds of exercise because _____.
    A. it develops strength more efficiently
    B. it demands less strength
    C. it is inexpensive
    D. it is trains the heart and lungs

15. Which is NOT mentioned as an advantage of excellent running shoes?
    A. Reduced injury.
    B. Reduced shock.
    C. Faster speed.
    D. Suitability for hard and soft surfaces.

16. In running one can wear _____.
    A. street clothes   B. expensive warm-up suits
    C. gym shorts   D. all of the above

17. Multi-layered clothing is preferred in cold weather because _____.
    A. it keeps the body warmer
    B. it is inexpensive and easy to wear
    C. it is easy to adapt to different conditions
    D. it can be worn in foul weather conditions

Questions 18 to 20 are based on the following passage. At the end of the passage, you will be given 15 seconds to answer the questions.

Now listen to the passage.

18. According to the passage, the advantage of mass advertising is _____.

A. lower prices

B. big demand for products

C. high-quality products

D. wise decision making by consumers

19. Which of the following is a rational buying motive?

A. Wanting to feel good.

B. Wanting to feel comfortable.

C. Feeling fear.

D. Feeling superior to your friends.

20. Companies believe that _____.

A. they should not spend too much money on advertising

B. consumers can make wise purchase decisions

C. their advertising will be effective

D. their advertising has strong rational appeals

SECTION C   NEWS BROADCAST

Questions 21 and 22 are based on the following news. At the end of the news item, you will be given 10 seconds to answer the questions.

Now listen to the news.

21. What did the storm first strike?

A. The eastern US.   B. The Gulf of Mexico.

C. The Canadian border.   D. Some areas in Cuba.

22. The storm has resulted in the following EXCEPT _____.

A. death and damage   B. disruption of air services

C. destruction of crops   D. relocation of people

Questions 23 and 24 are based on the following news. At the end of the news item, you will be given 10 seconds to answer the

questions.

Now listen to the news.

23. The emergency surgery was to _____.
    A. stabilize the heart   B. reduce brain pressure
    C. clean the brain wound   D. restore reparatory functions
24. The condition of Prime Minister Sharon can be described as

    _____.

    A. worse   B. fully recovered
    C. serious but stable   D. cannot be determined

Questions 25 *and* 26 *are based on the following news. At the end of the news item, you will be given* 10 *seconds to answer the questions.*

Now listen to the news.

25. The drug works by _____.
    A. keeping the viruses from entering cells
    B. combining the viruses with cells
    C. killing the viruses
    D. changing the chemical makeup of the viruses
26. A vaccine for SARS _____.
    A. is still some time away
    B. is impossible
    C. will be produced soon
    D. has been found already

Questions 27 *and* 28 *are based on the following news. At the end of the news item, you will be given* 10 *seconds to answer the questions.*

Now listen to the news.

27. Which of the following is most likely to be the cause of the plane crash?
    A. Pilot error.
    B. Sabotage（人为破坏）.
    C. Explosion.
    D. Weather.

28. The real cause of the plane crash _____.
    A. is already known
    B. is still unknown
    C. will soon be known
    D. will never be known

Questions 29 and 30 are based on the following news. At the end of the news item, you will be given 10 seconds to answer the questions.

Now listen to the news.

29. How many people were wounded?
    A. 1   B. 2   C. 3   D. 4

30. The attack affected _____.
    A. some airflights in Nairobi
    B. the normal work of a local hospital
    C. the return of refugees
    D. the election in Congo

PRACTICE TEST 3

PART I DICTATION [15 MIN.]

Listen to the following passage. Altogether the passage will be read to you four times. During the first reading, which will be read at normal speed, listen and try to understand the meaning. For the second and third readings, the passage will be read sentence by sentence, or phrase by phrase, with intervals of 15 seconds. The last reading will be read at normal speed again and during this time you should check your work. You will then be given 2 minutes to check through your work once more.

PART II LISTENING COMPREHENSION [15 MIN.]

In sections A, B and C you will hear everything once only. Listen carefully and then answer the questions that follow.

SECTION A CONVERSATIONS

In this section you will hear several conversations. Listen to the conversations carefully and then answer the questions that follow.

Questions 1 to 4 are based on the following conversation. At the end of the conversation, you will be given 20 seconds to answer the questions.

Now listen to the conversation.

1. Berry was shocked in Rio because _____.
   A. the beach was overcrowded
   B. travelers spent their time sleeping rather than sightseeing

26

C. people worked very hard while on vacation

D. there was a contrast between the rich and poor

2. What was the weather like?

A. The weather was good at the beginning of the visit.

B. The weather was bad at the beginning of the visit.

C. The weather was fine throughout Berry's visit.

D. The weather was bad throughout Berry's visit.

3. What was the food like?

A. It was inexpensive.

B. It consisted only of seafood.

C. Desert and drinks combined cost US$10.

D. The ten-dollar fixed fee cover everything.

4. What did Berry say about his visit?

A. It was a huge disappointment.

B. It was better than he had expected.

C. It was not what he had expected.

D. Cannot be determined from the conversation.

Questions 5 to 7 are based on the following conversation. At the end of the conversation, you will be given 20 seconds to answer the questions.

Now listen to the conversation.

5. Which of the following is NOT true of Victoria for this semester?

A. She will work harder.

B. She will not learn new course material.

C. She will get a degree.

D. She will prepare for her exams.

6. The reason Victoria lives with her aunt and uncle is that

_____.

A. she wants to save expenses

B. she likes socializing

C. she can go downtown easily

D. she can concentrate on her work

7. Which of the following is true?

    A. Victoria's tutor and lecturer are both very helpful.

    B. Victoria's tutor is helpful but not her lecturer.

    C. Victoria's lecturer is helpful but but not her tutor.

    D. Victoria believes that her tutor and lecturer should have done more for her.

Questions 8 to 10 are based on the following conversation. At the end of the conversation, you will be given 15 seconds to answer the questions.

Now listen to the conversation.

8. What do newspapers and radio and TV have in common?

    A. They are all objective.

    B. They all involve personalities.

    C. They all lack objectivity.

    D. They have the same impact on people.

9. Features of personality do not include _____.

    A. voice inflections (声调变化) B. exclamation marks

    C. facial expressions   D. body language

10. The two speakers seem to _____.

    A. have similar opinions   B. have different opinions

    C. agree only on certain points D. try to please each other

SECTION B PASSAGES

In this section, you will hear several passages. Listen to the passages carefully and then answer the questions that follow.

   Questions 11 to 13 are based on the following passage. At the end of the passage, you will be given 15 seconds to answer the questions.

   Now listen to the passage.

11. The main difference between high-quality and low-quality proteins lies in _____
    A. the number of essential amino acids
    B. the number of nonessential amino acids
    C. the number of the 20 amino acids
    D. the way the body uses them

12. Vegetarians should _____.
    A. eat some animal meat
    B. abandon their diet
    C. increase the amount of their diet
    D. expand the variety of their food

13. Which statement is true?
    A. The body does not need all the 20 amino acids to be healthy.
    B. Nonessential amino acids in our body come from plants.
    C. Low-quality proteins do not contain enough essential amino acids.
    D. Continued lack of proteins may cause poor health but will not cause death.

   Questions 14 to 17 are based on the following passage. At the end of the passage, you will be given 20 seconds to answer the questions.

   Now listen to the passage.

14. What makes Hong Kong, the Netherlands and Britain attractive places to do business?

   A. They used to suffer economic crises.

   B. They have good financial systems.

   C. They invest heavily overseas.

   D. They are having economic reforms.

15. What China needs to do is _____.

   A. emphasize the role of banks

   B. eliminate the role of banks

   C. rely solely on foreign investment

   D. expand the sources that provide money

16. All of the following are reasons that some countries have fallen behind EXCEPT _____.

   A. lack of natural resources

   B. lack of concentration of economic and political power

   C. lack of democratic systems

   D. poor financial systems

17. In the survey of capital markets, the United States takes the _____ place.

   A. third

   B. sixth

   C. ninth

   D. cannot be determined from the passage

Questions 18 *to* 20 *are based on the following passage. At the end of the passage, you will be given* 15 *seconds to answer the questions.*

   Now listen to the passage.

18. Which of the following is NOT true of love?

A. Love is everywhere.

B. Love is difficult to describe.

C. Love in its extreme form is not a problem.

D. Love is more researched than fear and anger

19. What do different kinds of love have in common?

    A. They can be negative sometimes.

    B. They involve other feelings.

    C. They are positive feelings toward others.

    D. They come from jealousy.

20. What does the passage say about hate?

    A. Hate is as positive as love.

    B. Hate is not a strong emotion.

    C. Hate is the worst of all emotions.

    D. Hate is not always a bad emotion.

SECTION C　NEWS BROADCAST

Questions 21 and 22 are based on the following news. At the end of the news item, you will be given 10 seconds to answer the questions.

Now listen to the news.

21. Shirin Ebadi is now a _____.

    A. politician   B. judge

    C. lawyer   D. teacher

22. Shirin Ebadi was awarded the Nobel Prize mainly for _____.

    A. her anti-war activities

    B. her work on political cases

    C. her work for people's rights

    D. her role in introducing Islamic law

31

Questions 23 to 25 are based on the following news. At the end of the news item, you will be given 15 seconds to answer the questions.

Now listen to the news.

23. The way Avastin works is similar to _____.
  A. cutting off enemy's supplying line
  B. bombing the enemy from air
  C. attacking the enemy when they are least alert
  D. weakening the enemy forces with sporadic attacks

24. For the moment, Avastin works effectively for _____.
  A. colon cancer
  B. breast cancer
  C. lung cancer
  D. liver cancer

25. Compared with chemotherapy, the new drug _____.
  A. kills more dividing cells
  B. has more side effects
  C. chooses targets more accurately
  D. is more powerful

Questions 26 and 27 are based on the following news. At the end of the news item, you will be given 10 seconds to answer the questions.

Now listen to the news.

26. What has happened to Michael Eisner?
  A. He has lost all of his positions.
  B. He has become the new chairman of Walt Disney.
  C. He has retained part of his previous positions
  D. He has escaped a crisis unscathed.

27. The shareholders believe that _____.

A. George Mitchell is a lot worse than Michael Eisner

B. George Mitchell is much better than Michael Eisner

C. George Mitchell may not bring change to Walt Disney

D. George Mitchell and Michael Eisner have been rivals with each other

Questions 28 and 29 are based on the following news. At the end of the news item, you will be given 10 seconds to answer the questions.

Now listen to the news.

28. The new technology involves the sense of _____.

    A. touch   B. smell

    C. taste   D. sound

29. 2. The research of the new technology can be described as _____.

    A. wrong   B. unrealistic

    C. mature   D. highly possible

Question 30 is based on the following news. At the end of the news item, you will be given 5 seconds to answer the question.

Now listen to the news.

30. The news is mainly about _____.

    A. the origin of Ebola viruses in humans

    B. the treatment of Ebola viruses

    C. Ebola viruses in animals

    D. the consequence of Ebola viruses

PRACTICE TEST 4

PART I   DICTATION   [15 MIN.]

*Listen to the following passage. Altogether the passage will be
read to you four times. During the first reading, which will be
read at normal speed, listen and try to understand the meaning. For
the second and third readings, the passage will be read sentence by
sentence, or phrase by phrase, with intervals of 15 seconds. The last
reading will be read at normal speed again and during this time you
should check your work. You will then be given 2 minutes to check
through your work once more.*

PART II   LISTENING COMPREHENSION   [15 MIN.]

*In sections A, B and C you will hear everything once only.
Listen carefully and then answer the questions that follow.*

SECTION A   CONVERSATIONS

*In this section you will hear several conversations. Listen to the
conversations carefully and then answer the questions that follow.*

*Questions 1 to 3 are based on the following conversation. At the
end of the conversation, you will be given 15 seconds to answer the
questions.*

Now listen to the conversation.

1. Which of the following is NOT a reason that Miss Lauren missed
   class discussions?
   A. She doesn't believe class discussions are very useful.
   B. The topics are too difficult.

34

C. The topics are not well prepared.

D. She finds it difficult to get the chance to speak.

2. Professor Walter believes that in class discussions one should

　　　　　.

A. learn how to dominate a conversation

B. take a back seat and let others speak more

C. be as polite and sensitive as possible

D. be aggressive and speak up

3. Miss Lauren likes topics that 　　　　.

A. relate to her personal experiences

B. do not relate to the subjects she is learning

C. are prepared by students rather than professors

D. encourage independent study

Questions 4 to 7 are based on the following conversation. At the end of the conversation, you will be given 20 seconds to answer the questions.

Now listen to the conversation.

4. What does Jason say about "a friend in need is a friend indeed?"

A. It is the most important principle for friendship.

B. It is not enough as a principle for friendship.

C. It is outdated and is no longer important.

D. It is forgotten as a principle for friendship.

5. Jason makes friends 　　　　.

A. extensively   B. selectively

C. only with men   D. only with women

6. Eileen believes that true friendship 　　　　.

A. is like love   B. lasts a long time

C. never exists   D. exists within marriage

7. What does Eileen say about online friendship?
   A. It may not be real.　　　　B. It is based on honesty.
   C. It is more exciting.　　　 D. It lasts a long time.

Questions 8 to 10 are based on the following conversation. At the end of the conversation, you will be given 15 seconds to answer the questions.

Now listen to the conversation.

8. Which is NOT Mr. Lewis' purpose of the visit.
   A. To visit friends.　　　　　B. To give concerts.
   C. To vacation.　　　　　　　D. To give private lessons.
9. What kind of cello did Mr. Lewis use when he was eight?
   A. A full-sized cello.　　　　 B. A half-sized cello.
   C. A two-thirds-sized cello.　 D. It is not mentioned.
10. Which is true of Mr. Lewis's cello?
    A. It sometimes accompanies him on his trips.
    B. It is left behind when he goes on a trip.
    C. It incurs extra expenses.
    D. It is difficult for him to carry it around.

SECTION B　PASSAGES

In this section, you will hear several passages. Listen to the passages carefully and then answer the questions that follow.

Questions 11 to 13 are based on the following passage. At the end of the passage, you will be given 15 seconds to answer the questions.

Now listen to the passage.

11. The passage is mainly about _____.

A. the ways to keep eye contact

B. the cultural differences of eye contact

C. the physical properties of eye contact

D. the functions of eye contact

12. In conversations we maintain eye contact when we _____.

    A. are paying attention   B. are making some request

    C. are seeking approval   D. all of these

13. Eyes can communicate _____.

    A. our status   B. the skill of conversation

    C. our feelings   D. our identity

Questions 14 *to* 17 *are based on the following passage. At the end of the passage, you will be given* 20 *seconds to answer the questions.*

Now listen to the passage.

14. Which is the second most important foreign language in the European Union?

    A. English   B. German.

    C. Dutch.   D. French.

15. What is true of the Luxembourgeois?

    A. They can hardly speak a foreign language.

    B. Most of them can speak foreign languages.

    C. Their native language is being replaced by foreign languages.

    D. They only speak French as a foreign language.

16. What is true of the French?

    A. Half of them accept English as a foreign language.

    B. A majority of them still resist English as a foreign language.

    C. A majority of them accept English as a working language.

    D. A third of them accept English as a working language.

17. What does the passage say about English in the European Union?
   A. English is the working language at administrative and business levels.
   B. English will soon become the official language.
   C. It is still some time before English can be accepted by professional classes.
   D. English is unifying the countries in the European Union.

Questions 18 *to* 20 *are based on the following passage. At the end of the passage, you will be given* 15 *seconds to answer the questions.*

Now listen to the passage.

18. Which is NOT a true fact?
   A. Suicide kills more people aged 15~34 in China than anything else.
   B. China's suicide rates are very high compared with many other countries.
   C. Suicides tend to be committed by young, rural women.
   D. The number of people committing suicide in China is very large.
19. According to Dr. Phillips, one reason that in China more women commit suicide than men is that _____.
   A. women are discriminated against
   B. women have limited education
   C. women are more successful at killing themselves
   D. more women attempt suicide
20. According to Dr. Phillips, suicides in China are caused by _____.
   A. mental illness only

B. poverty only

C. conflicts and school failure only

D. other factors besides mental illness

SECTION C   NEWS BROADCST

Question 21 is based on the following news. At the end of the
news item, you will be given 5 seconds to answer the questions.
Now listen to the news.

21. The AIDS problem is _____ .

    A. becoming worse   B. stable temporarily

    C. improving slightly   D. expected to improve shortly

Questions 22 and 23 are based on the following news. At the end
of the news item, you will be given 10 seconds to answer the questions
Now listen to the news.

22. What is true of the game between Australia and India? :

    A. India once led by a score of 2:0.

    B. Australia once led by a score of 4:0.

    C. Australia scored its goals in the last ten minutes.

    D. Australia scored six goals.

23. Which team is in the third position at the moment?

    A. Australia.   B. Pakistan.

    C. South Korea.   D. Germany.

Questions 24 and 25 are based on the following news. At the end
of the news item, you will be given 10 seconds to answer the
questions.
Now listen to the news.

24. The two British men were _____.
    A. sent into prison   B. sexually abused
    C. lost their children   D. fined for speeding
25. A committee will be discussing _____.
    A. how much money should be fined
    B. how to use the fines to help the victims
    C. how many shelters will be built
    D. who will appear in court to testify

Questions 26 and 27 are based on the following news. At the end of the news item, you will be given 10 seconds to answer the questions.

Now listen to the news.

26. The crash is _____.
    A. is successful   B. is unsuccessful
    C. is not what was expected D. is less powerful than expected
27. The crash could shed light on _____.
    A. actual size of our universe
    B. the lifespan of our solar system
    C. the original makeup of our solar system
    D. the number of comets near our solar system

Questions 28 to 30 are based on the following news. At the end of the news item, you will be given 15 seconds to answer the questions.

Now listen to the news.

28. The best title for the news is _____.

40

A. A Traditional View Challenged

B. Water—Enemy of Cold

C. Cold— an Incurable Disease

D. A New Solution to Treating Cold

29. There is evidence that during respiratory infections _____.

    A. drinking water will reduce the symptoms

    B. drinking water can keep salt in the body

    C. water is conserved in the body

    D. drinking water will produce more salt in the body

30. Researchers believe that higher fluid consumption during a respiratory illness _____.

    A. should be recommended

    B. should not be recommended at all

    C. need no further medical research

    D. should be handled with caution

PRACTICE TEST 5

PART I   DICTATION   [15 MIN.]

Listen to the following passage. Altogether the passage will be read to you four times. During the first reading, which will be read at normal speed, listen and try to understand the meaning. For the second and third readings, the passage will be read sentence by sentence, or phrase by phrase, with intervals of 15 seconds. The last reading will be read at normal speed again and during this time you should check your work. You will then be given 2 minutes to check through your work once more.

PART II   LISTENING COMPREHENSION   [15 MIN.]

In sections A, B and C you will hear everything once only. Listen carefully and then answer the questions that follow.

SECTION A   CONVERSATIONS

In this section you will hear several conversations. Listen to the conversations carefully and then answer the questions that follow.

Questions 1 to 3 are based on the following conversation. At the end of the conversation, you will be given 15 seconds to answer the questions.

Now listen to the conversation.

1. What does Lisa say about her college study?
   A. She follows a tight schedule.
   B. She is good at formal exams.
   C. She takes her course work seriously.

42

D. The course work does not suit her.

2. What does Lisa say about her work placement?

   A. Her work placement lasts a week.

   B. She gets paid for her work placement.

   C. Her work placement gives her some time for leisure.

   D. Her tutors are strict and demanding.

3. Lisa implies that _____.

   A. she doesn't like her college study very much

   B. her tutor decides everything for her

   C. she wants to explore some better ways to attend college

   D. she likes her study because of the freedom she enjoys

   Questions 4 *to* 7 *are based on the following conversation. At the end of the conversation, you will be given* 20 *seconds to answer the questions.*

   Now listen to the conversation.

4. Americans tend to _____.

   A. be confident in stating their views

   B. disregard other people's views

   C. disregard their own achievements

   D. selfish and greedy

5. Americans care about personal space because _____.

   A. they can be turned off by body odor

   B. they are taller and bigger

   C. they don't enjoy intimate relationship

   D. they believe the relationship is not intimate enough

6. Casual acquaintances should avoid all of the following forms of physical contact with Americans EXCEPT _____.

   A. shaking hands momentarily

B. holding their hands

C. putting your arm around their shoulder

D. touching their faces

7. Americans are _____ eye contact.

   A. disrespectful about   B. suspicious of

   C. fine with   D. afraid of

Questions 8 to 10 are based on the following conversation. At the end of the conversation, you will be given 15 seconds to answer the questions.

Now listen to the conversation.

8. Warren didn't like the movie because _____.

   A. it told a very simple story

   B. it was a light movie

   C. it featured non-traditional dialogue

   D. the director was too traditional

9. What does Cathy mean when she says she prefers movies with substance?

   A. She prefers movies of gunfights and car chasing.

   B. She prefers mainstream movies.

   C. She prefers movies that are thought-provoking

   D. She prefers movies that make you relax.

10. Cathy and Warren agree on _____.

    A. the mystery movie they saw

    B. the artistic value of the movie they saw last night

    C. mainstream movies

    D. the director of the movie they saw last night

SECTION B PASSAGES

In this section, you will hear several passages. Listen to the passages carefully and then answer the questions that follow.

Questions 11 to 13 are based on the following passage. At the end of the passage, you will be given 15 seconds to answer the questions.

Now listen to the passage.

11. Animals move from place to place so that _____.
    A. food can be shared among animals
    B. animals can eat different kinds of food
    C. old food sources can recover
    D. different animals can live together

12. The new problem is that _____.
    A. cattle destroy food supply
    B. wild animals ferociously attack cattle
    C. cattle occupy the traditional habitats of wild animals
    D. wild animals no longer move from place to place

13. Wild animals and cattle differ in _____.
    A. the amount of grass and plants they eat
    B. the way they eat grass and plants
    C. the type of grass and plants they eat
    D. the time they spend eating grass and plants

Questions 14 to 17 are based on the following passage. At the end of the passage, you will be given 20 seconds to answer the questions.

Now listen to the passage.

14. BBC's weather forecast is a _____ program.
    A. seldom watched   B. little known
    C. new   D. popular
15. Weather observations come from all the sources EXCEPT
    _____.
    A. computers   B. satellites
    C. the ground   D. radar
16. What does the passage say about BBC's forecasters?
    A. They read from a script.
    B. They are professionals.
    C. They use a map for presentation.
    D. They care about their clothes.
17. What does the passage say about British television viewers?
    A. They remember what they saw on weather forecasts.
    B. They like talking about weather instead of watching.
    C. They pay more attention to the style of the presenters.
    D. They watch and remember what is necessary.

Questions 18 *to* 20 *are based on the following passage. At the end of the passage, you will be given* 15 *seconds to answer the questions.*
    Now listen to the passage.

18. The passage mentions the following as causes of heart disease in developing nations EXCEPT _____.
    A. the costly living in big cities
    B. people eating more food than necessary
    C. more frequent smoking
    D. lack of exercise
19. Which country has the lowest heart disease rate?

46

A. India.
B. Brazil.
C. The United States.
D. China.

20. What does the passage say about the impact of heart disease in developing nations?

   A. Heart disease brings political and social instability.

   B. Heart disease is especially hard on old people.

   C. Heart disease makes prevention and treatment difficult.

   D. Heart disease weakens labor productivity.

SECTION C   NEWS BROADCAST

Questions 21 to 23 are based on the following news. At the end of the news item, you will be given 15 seconds to answer the questions.

Now listen to the news.

21. The woman was attacked when _____.

   A. she was driving

   B. she got into the car of a man

   C. she was walking at night

   D. she was asking the way

22. What did the woman do when she was being attacked?

   A. Drove the car to the police.

   B. Bit the man's fingers

   C. Shouted at the passing cars.

   D. Beat the man with a stick.

23. Which of the following is NOT true of the man?

   A. He was in his 20s and 30s.

   B. He drove a silver car.

   C. He had a large nose.

   D. He spoke with a Scottish accent.

Questions 24 *and* 25 *are based on the following news. At the end of the news item, you will be given* 10 *seconds to answer the questions.*

Now listen to the news.

24. The two men were killed when _____.
    A. they were being chased by police
    B. a bus turned over their car
    C. they were getting away after stealing the car
    D. they were fired by police
25. How many people received treatment at the scene for shock?
    A. 2   B. 3   C. 4   D. 5

Questions 26 *and* 27 *are based on the following news. At the end of the news item, you will be given* 10 *seconds to answer the questions.*

Now listen to the news.

26. Which is NOT true of the woman?
    A. She had a chicken farm.
    B. She did not kill her chicken as ordered by the government.
    C. She died of a fever.
    D. She had close contact with bird flu patients.
27. The bird flu virus _____.
    A. has killed 9 people in Egypt
    B. can infect people in close contact with birds
    C. are transmitted from human to human
    D. is not a deadly virus

48

Questions 28 *and* 29 *are based on the following news. At the end of the news item, you will be given* 10 *seconds to answer the questions.*

Now listen to the news.

28. What is required for the Kyoto Treaty to begin to take effect?
    A. The number of countries.
    B. The ratification by both the US and Russia.
    C. The economic power of countries that ratify the treaty.
    D. The percentage of emissions.

29. Russia's role in passing the treaty is _____.
    A. overstated   B. negligible
    C. vital   D. not very important

Question 30 *is based on the following news. At the end of the news item, you will be given* 5 *seconds to answer the question.*

Now listen to the news.

30. The news is mainly about _____.
    A. protection of drug patents
    B. manufacturing drugs in poor countries
    C. WTO's role in fighting diseases
    D. poor countries' access to cheap drugs

PRACTICE TEST 6

PART I DICTATION [15 MIN.]

Listen to the following passage. Altogether the passage will be read to you four times. During the first reading, which will be read at normal speed, listen and try to understand the meaning. For the second and third readings, the passage will be read sentence by sentence, or phrase by phrase, with intervals of 15 seconds. The last reading will be read at normal speed again and during this time you should check your work. You will then be given 2 minutes to check through your work once more.

PART II LISTENING COMPREHENSION [15 MIN.]

In sections A, B and C you will hear everything once only. Listen carefully and then answer the questions that follow.

SECTION A CONVERSATIONS

In this section you will hear several conversations. Listen to the conversations carefully and then answer the questions that follow.

Questions 1 to 3 are based on the following conversation. At the end of the conversation, you will be given 15 seconds to answer the questions.

Now listen to the conversation.

1. Both Terry and Emily _____.
   A. drink only during the week
   B. drink only at weekends
   C. drink more at weekends than during the week

D. drink every night

2. A "unit" is a measurement of _____.

    A. how much a woman should drink

    B. how much a man should drink

    C. the volume of a drink

    D. the strength of a drink

3. The maximum amount of alcohol a man can drink a day is _____ units.

    A. 4   B. 10   C. 15   D. 20

Questions 4 to 7 are based on the following conversation. At the end of the conversation, you will be given 20 seconds to answer the questions.

Now listen to the conversation.

4. Terry was impressed with _____.

    A. a bridge to Manhattan   B. skyscrapers at dusk

    C. streets in Manhattan   D. people in Manhattan

5. What does Terry say about the garbage in New York?

    A. Smelly.

    B. Scattered.

    C. Blocking doors and store shutters.

    D. Put in bags and boxes.

6. The hotel Terry stayed at can be described as _____.

    A. roomy and comfortable   B. decent but expensive

    C. cheap and comfortable   D. roomy but expensive

7. Terry's impression of New York could be characterized by _____.

    A. orderliness   B. creativeness

    C. narrow space   D. convenience

Questions 8 to 10 are based on the following conversation. At the end of the conversation, you will be given 15 seconds to answer the questions.

Now listen to the conversation.

8. The elephant can be described as _____.
   A. playful
   B. ferocious（凶恶的）
   C. slow
   D. thoughtful

9. Terry tried his best to _____.
   A. stare back at the elephant
   B. roll over the ground
   C. hold the tusks
   D. hit the elephant in the eyes

10. The encounter with the elephant can be described as _____.
    A. very dangerous
    B. not risky
    C. exciting
    D. funny

SECTION B   PASSAGES

In this section, you will hear several passages. Listen to the passages carefully and then answer the questions that follow.

Questions 11 to 13 are based on the following passage. At the end of the passage, you will be given 15 seconds to answer the questions.

Now listen to the passage.

11. The passage says that the chameleon spends most of its time
    _____.
    A. changing its color
    B. sitting motionless
    C. moving slowly
    D. moving its eyes

12. According to the passage, the slow motion of the chameleon is
_____.
   A. an attacking scheme   B. a disappointment
   C. a threat to the chameleon   D. a protective device
13. The naked human eye can NOT see _____.
   A. the chameleon opening its mouth
   B. the chameleon shooting out its tongue
   C. the chameleon taking back its tongue
   D. the chameleon's jaw snapping shut

   Questions 14 *to* 17 *are based on the following passage. At the
end of the passage, you will be given* 20 *seconds to answer the
questions.*
   Now listen to the passage.

14. Our clothes can _____.
   A. tell who we are
   B. improve our communicative skills
   C. cultivate our values
   D. control our lifestyles
15. Traditionally men _____.
   A. cared little about clothing
   B. had poor taste about clothing
   C. were very conscious about clothing
   D. were proud of women's clothes
16. What is true of blue-collar workers according to the research of
1955?
   A. They cared more about clothing than white-collar workers.
   B. They were manipulated by white-collar workers.
   C. They ridiculed white-collar workers for their clothing.

D. They conformed to the accepted pattern of clothing.

17. According to the passage, what has changed since 1955?

    A. The importance of clothing.

    B. The relationship between white-collar and blue-collar workers.

    C. The pattern of dress.

    D. The cost of dress.

Questions 18 *to* 20 *are based on the following passage. At the end of the passage, you will be given* 15 *seconds to answer the questions.*

Now listen to the passage.

18. A driver who violates the ban for the fifth time will be fined _____.

    A. $100   B. $200

    C. $500   D. none of these

19. Which is NOT a true statement?

    A. New York State is the first state to have passed the ban on cell-phone use by motorists.

    B. New York State's ban on cell-phone use by motorists is the first in the country.

    C. Some states other than New York have proposed bans on cell-phone use by motorists.

    D. Some countries have laws banning cell-phone use by motorists.

20. Critics believe that the ban _____.

    A. is too severe

    B. is difficult to carry out

    C. targets only one area of unsafe driving

D. contributes to accidents on the road

SECTION C NEWS BROADCAST

Question 21 *is based on the following news. At the end of the news item, you will be given* 5 *seconds to answer the question.*
  Now listen to the news.

21. Scientists from South Korea have successfully _____.
    A. cloned a human being
    B. treated diseases with cloned cells
    C. cloned human stem cells
    D. transplanted cloned cells

Questions 22 *and* 23 *are based on the following news. At the end of the news item, you will be given* 10 *seconds to answer the questions.*
  Now listen to the news.

22. The news is mainly about _____.
    A. the spread of mad cow disease in the US
    B. the treatment of mad cow disease in the US
    C. a suspected case of mad cow disease in the US
    D. the testing of mad cow disease in the US
23. We can infer from the news that _____.
    A. mad cow disease is likely to spread in the US
    B. Britain once had the spread of mad cow disease
    C. it is difficult to confirm a case of mad cow disease
    D. the US will not have a mad cow disease

Questions 24 *to* 26 *are based on the following news. At the end*

55

of the news item, you will be given 15 *seconds to answer the questions.*

Now listen to the news.

24. US productivity fell 0. 6% in the _____ quarter of 2005.
   A. first   B. second   C. third   D. fourth
25. According to economists, the decline in productivity could be attributed to _____.
   A. trade deficit   B. natural disaster
   C. inflation   D. world economy
26. In 2005, salary growth _____.
   A. increased slightly   B. increased sharply
   C. dropped sharply   D. none of these

Questions 27 *and* 28 *are based on the following news. At the end of the news item, you will be given* 10 *seconds to answer the questions.*

Now listen to the news.

27. NASA _____ that there used to be water on Mars.
   A. is certain   B. speculates
   C. is doubtful   D. denies
28. What did the robotic probe Opportunity do?
   A. It looked for hot springs.
   B. It looked for traces of life in a lakebed
   C. It looked for ice.
   D. It studied the makeup of a rock

Questions 29 *and* 30 *are based on the following news. At the end of the news item, you will be given* 10 *seconds to answer the*

56

questions.

    Now listen to the news.

29. Australia reacted towards the French test by _____.
    A. recalling her ambassador to Paris
    B. describing the test as insignificant
    C. expressing her regret
    D. expressing disapproval
30. French President Jacque Chirac said that his country might carry out _____ nuclear test(s).
    A. one   B. fewer than 8
    C. 8   D. more than 8

PRACTICE TEST 7

PART I   DICTATION   [15 MIN.]

Listen to the following passage. Altogether the passage will be read to you four times. During the first reading, which will be read at normal speed, listen and try to understand the meaning. For the second and third readings, the passage will be read sentence by sentence, or phrase by phrase, with intervals of 15 seconds. The last reading will be read at normal speed again and during this time you should check your work. You will then be given 2 minutes to check through your work once more.

PART II   LISTENING COMPREHENSION   [15 MIN.]

In sections A, B and C you will hear everything once only. Listen carefully and then answer the questions that follow.

SECTION A   CONVERSATIONS

In this section you will hear several conversations. Listen to the conversations carefully and then answer the questions that follow.

Questions 1 to 3 are based on the following conversation. At the end of the conversation, you will be given 15 seconds to answer the questions.

Now listen to the conversation.

1. What is considered bad manners in South Korea?
   A. Eating one's food slowly.
   B. Eating one's food quickly.
   C. Wearing white socks with suits

58

D. Wearing white ties with suits

2. All of the following are bad manners in Malaysia EXCEPT
    _____.
    A. eating food too loudly
    B. eating before the guests are served
    C. keeping too close a personal space
    D. serving guests too much food

3. It is strange in Japan that _____.
    A. people cannot kiss in parks
    B. people can kiss anywhere
    C. people can only kiss in parks
    D. people carry magazines when they have a date

    Questions 4 to 7 are based on the following conversation. At the
end of the conversation, you will be given 20 seconds to answer the
questions.
    Now listen to the conversation.

4. Which of the following is true of Laura?
    A. She has a low opinion of her looks.
    B. She cares very much about her weight.
    C. She doesn't care about her appearance.
    D. She thinks that she is very fat.

5. Which of the following words best describes the efforts made by
    both Laura's mother and her grandmother to reduce weight?
    A. Innovative.   B. Persistent.
    C. Futile.   D. Conservative.

6. Laura's problem can be attributed to her _____.
    A. eating poor food   B. sleeping too early
    C. being lazy   D. eating too much

7. Laura believes that _____.
   A. she has stronger will than other people
   B. it is difficult for her not to eat more
   C. she has some genetic disease
   D. she can eat but does not gain weight

Questions 8 to 10 are based on the following conversation. At the end of the conversation, you will be given 15 seconds to answer the questions.

Now listen to the conversation.

8. To call teachers by their first names _____.
   A. is not problem for foreign students
   B. is a problem for all foreign students
   C. is a problem for most foreign students
   D. is a problem for some foreign students
9. The chairs and tables are organized in a way that _____.
   A. motivates students
   B. facilitates student participation
   C. makes lessons easier to understand
   D. teachers can closely monitor students' activities
10. American teachers _____ punctuality.
   A. are informal about   B. dislikes
   C. don't understand   D. care about

SECTION B   PASSAGES

In this section, you will hear several passages. Listen to the passages carefully and then answer the questions that follow.

Questions 11 to 13 are based on the following passage. At the end of the passage, you will be given 15 seconds to answer the

questions.

Now listen to the passage.

11. The cat skeleton found in Cyprus dates back to about _____ years.
    A. 9,000   B. 5,000
    C. 4,000   D. 1,000
12. The new finding _____.
    A. confirms the known date of cats as pets
    B. Disproves cats as human pets
    C. provides proof for a long-time speculation
    D. is strongly disputed by some scientists
13. Which is NOT true of the cat skeleton?
    A. It was buried together with the skeleton of a human.
    B. It was buried as an offering.
    C. It shows no sign of brutal killing.
    D. It looks similar to the skeleton of a wild cat.

Questions 14 to 17 are based on the following passage. At the end of the passage, you will be given 20 seconds to answer the questions.

Now listen to the passage.

14. One purpose of writing a letter of complaint to a vendor is to _____.
    A. tell him that there is a problem
    B. accuse him of irresponsibility
    C. accuse him of negligence
    D. tell him that his company is a total failure
15. The preferred way of making a vendor answer your complaint is

to _____.

A. take legal action against him whenever possible

B. make him feel shameful

C. make him feel obliged and willing to do something for you

D. tell him the possible consequences

16. A letter of complaint should do all of the following EXCEPT

_____.

A. sound polite but resolute

B. present hard facts

C. make clear your request

D. do not tell the consequences of the problem

17. A successful letter of complaint is one that _____ the vendor.

A. entertains   B. condones

C. praises   D. motivates

Questions 18 *to* 20 *are based on the following passage. At the end of the passage, you will be given* 15 *seconds to answer the questions.*

Now listen to the passage.

18. Vitamin E deficiency _____.

A. will cause some adults to suffer anemia

B. cannot be detected in normal tests

C. will produce premature infants

D. produces few symptoms in humans

19. Producers of deodorants that contain vitamin E believe that vitamin E _____.

A. kills bacteria

B. prevents sweat from being oxidized

C. oxidizes bacteria

D. traps odor in the body

20. We can conclude from the passage that _____.

    A. vitamin E is only helpful in preventing heart disease

    B. vitamin E is dangerous to health

    C. people should use vitamin E in their diet

    D. claims for the uses of vitamin E are not scientifically proved

SECTION C   NEWS BROADCAST

Questions 21and 22 are based on the following news. At the end of the news item, you will be given 10 seconds to answer the questions.

Now listen to the news.

21. The cyclone did all of the following EXCEPT _____.

    A. made many people homeless

    B. cut off power

    C. damage many homes

    D. caused deaths

22. The injuries caused by the cyclone are _____.

    A. extensive   B. serious

    C. minor   D. not known

Questions 23 and 24 are based on the following news. At the end of the news item, you will be given 10 seconds to answer the questions.

Now listen to the news.

23. The study shows that _____.

    A. old women drink more than old men

    B. middle-aged women drink more than middle-aged men

C. young women drink more than young men

D. teenage girls drink more than teenage boys

24. In the past women drank less than men possibly because

_____.

A. women cared about social opinions

B. women had less money than men to buy drinks

C. women didn't have the need to drink

D. women cared more about their health

Questions 25 and 26 are based on the following news. At the end of the news item, you will be given 10 seconds to answer the questions.

Now listen to the news.

25. The health of Australia's indigenous people _____.

A. is improving

B. is horrible

C. is better than that of people in poor countries

D. is not as bad as people think

26. Which of the following is LEAST likely to improve aboriginal health?

A. Better housing. B. More nutritious food.

C. More health care. D. More education.

Question 27 is based on the following news. At the end of the news item, you will be given 5 seconds to answer the question.

Now listen to the news.

27. What will General Motor do?

A. To borrow money from the government.

B. To cut cost.

C. To reduce the loss to 3. 8 billion dollars.

D. To avoid direct competition with Asian rivals.

Questions 28 to 30 are based on the following news. At the end of the news item, you will be given 15 seconds to answer the questions.

Now listen to the news.

28. About _____ percent of foreign-owned companies avoided federal taxes altogether.

　　A. 10　　　　B. 35　　　　C. 60　　　　D. 70

29. The federal tax rate on corporations is _____ percent.

　　A. 25　　　　　　　　　B. 35

　　C. 45　　　　　　　　　D. not mentioned in the news

30. Evading taxes by corporations in America is _____.

　　A. not as serious as people think

　　B. a thing of the past

　　C. an established practice

　　D. approved by the general public

PRACTICE TEST 8

PART I   DICTATION   [15 MIN.]

Listen to the following passage. Altogether the passage will be read to you four times. During the first reading, which will be read at normal speed, listen and try to understand the meaning. For the second and third readings, the passage will be read sentence by sentence, or phrase by phrase, with intervals of 15 seconds. The last reading will be read at normal speed again and during this time you should check your work. You will then be given 2 minutes to check through your work once more.

PART II   LISTENING COMPREHENSION   [15 MIN.]

In sections A, B and C you will hear everything once only. Listen carefully and then answer the questions that follow.

SECTION A   CONVERSATIONS

In this section you will hear several conversations. Listen to the conversations carefully and then answer the questions that follow.

Questions 1 to 3 are based on the following conversation. At the end of the conversation, you will be given 15 seconds to answer the questions.

Now listen to the conversation.

1. What is the present status of literature?
    A. It is abandoned completely.
    B. It is no longer essential.
    C. It is far less valued than sports or movies.

D. It is no longer useful in cultivating good manners.

2. According to the conversation, literature makes it possible for people to _____.
   A. understand that they have much in common
   B. realize that they are ordinary people
   C. see that they can understand Shakespeare or Tolstoy
   D. be aware that they live in different circumstances

3. According to the conversation, literature can let people _____.
   A. challenge the existing conditions
   B. be critical about literary works
   C. have a strong sense of happiness
   D. see their lives positively

Questions 4 to 7 are based on the following conversation. At the end of the conversation, you will be given 20 seconds to answer the questions.

Now listen to the conversation.

4. According Susan, Larry should _____.
   A. look at college as an extension of high school
   B. keep what he has been
   C. pretend what he is not
   D. change himself

5. According to Susan, Larry should bring a camera with him because _____.
   A. he can send photos to his date of high school
   B. he can request money from his family
   C. he can make some money by taking photos for others
   D. he can make a photo album

6. A microwave and a mini-fridge are useful in that _____.

A. Larry doesn't have to go to the cafeteria all the time

B. Larry can learn how to cook on his own

C. Larry can cook more nutritious food than is provided in the cafeteria

D. cafeterias don't cater to students

7. According to Susan, Larry should _____.

A. stay with his high school mate

B. explore in college new relationships other than his high school date

C. have as many dates as possible

D. stop dating in college

Questions 8 to 10 are based on the following conversation. At the end of the conversation, you will be given 20 seconds to answer the questions.

Now listen to the conversation.

8. All of the following are true of Alan EXCEPT _____.

A. he has a strong interest in celebrities

B. he holds celebrities as role models

C. he imitates the lifestyles of celebrities

D. he get inspirations from celebrities

9. According to Karen, all of the following are true EXCEPT _____.

A. celebrities are no more ideal citizens than we are

B. celebrities make us spend money

C. people should not have any interest in celebrities

D. we should care more about our friends and families than celebrities

10. Karen and Alan seem to agree most on _____.

68

A. interest in celebrities

B. inspirational values of celebrities

C. the entertainment value of celebrities

D. celebrities as role models

SECTION B　PASSAGES

In this section, you will hear several passages. Listen to the passages carefully and then answer the questions that follow.

Questions 11 to 13 are based on the following passage. At the end of the passage, you will be given 15 seconds to answer the questions.

Now listen to the passage.

11. Americans will find Korean dating services _____ .

    A. surprising   B. innovative

    C. old-fashioned   D. sophisticated

12. The reason that people didn't bother about romantic love in the past is largely _____ .

    A. cultural   B. moral

    C. economic   D. political

13. The majority of college students believe that love _____ .

    A. is one of the desirable qualities in a mate

    B. is the least important qualities in a mate

    C. is the only quality in a mate

    D. none of these

Questions 14 to 17 are based on the following passage. At the end of the passage, you will be given 20 seconds to answer the questions.

Now listen to the passage.

14. What is true of women drivers?

    A. They can't drive competently.

    B. They are not always good drivers.

    C. They always cause deadly accidents.

    D. Their driving is no cause for concern.

15. What is true of a wise male driver?

    A. He is confident about women drivers.

    B. He is frightened by women drivers.

    C. He knows that women drivers are better than himself.

    D. He is always alert about women drivers.

16. When women talk, they _____.

    A. don't listen very carefully

    B. use more words than necessary

    C. interpret each other through facial expressions

    D. distract each other from their talk

17. Unlike men, women drivers _____.

    A. can't handle mechanical complexities

    B. are afraid of driving

    C. don't feel satisfaction about driving

    D. believe in safe driving

Questions 18 to 20 are based on the following passage. At the end of the passage, you will be given 15 seconds to answer the questions.

Now listen to the passage.

18. Which is true of arranged marriage in India?

    A. It is widely practiced.

    B. It exists in certain classes.

70

C. It is limited by languages.

D. It has met some strong resistance.

19. A bride is desirable if she _____.

    A. can become a good wife

    B. is capable of love and care

    C. has been tested for long-term marriage

    D. suits the big family's temperament or background

20. Which is the LEAST important quality for a young Indian man?

    A. Personality.   B. Education.

    C. Potential earning power. D. The social status of his family.

SECTION C   NEWS BROADCAST

Question 21 is based on the following news. At the end of the news item, you will be given 5 seconds to answer the question.

Now listen to the news.

21. Before April, the number of people who will get food ration is

    _____.

    A. 6 million   B. 1.5 million

    C. 500,000   D. 100,000

Questions 22 and 23 are based on the following news. At the end of the news item, you will be given 10 seconds to answer the questions.

Now listen to the news.

22. Which of the following is true of the education for children, especially girls, in the world?

    A. There has been little improvement over the years.

    B. There will be great improvement in the near future.

C. In some countries there is deterioration after a general improvement.

D. It has remained the same for decades.

23. According to the news, what is the reason that some children miss primary school education?

A. They have become AIDS patients.

B. They can't afford the expenses of education.

C. They are preoccupied by AIDS-related problems.

D. There is widespread exploitation of child labor.

Questions 24 and 25 are based on the following news. At the end of the news item, you will be given 10 seconds to answer the questions.

Now listen to the news.

24. By the end of next year, Wal-Mart will have _____ stores in China.

A. 20	B. 56
C. 76	D. 100

25. Which of the following is the largest foreign retailer in China?

A. Wal-Mart	B. Carrefour
C. Metro	D. Tesco

Questions 26 and 27 are based on the following news. At the end of the news item, you will be given 10 seconds to answer the questions.

Now listen to the news.

26. The news is mainly about _____.

A. Russian President Putin's visit to China

B. building oil pipelines in Siberia

C. sending gas from Russia to China

D. military cooperation between China and Russia

27. China and Russia signed _____ agreements relating to the energy sector.

A. 4   B. 5   C. 8   D. 15

Questions 28 to 30 are based on the following news. At the end of the news item, you will be given 15 seconds to answer the questions.

Now listen to the news.

28. The main idea of the news is that _____.

A. ending child labor incurs little cost

B. ending child labor does not bring benefits in the long run

C. the economic benefits of ending child labor outweigh the cost

D. ending child labor is a daunting talk

29. The cost of ending child labor is about _____.

A. four trillion dollars

B. one trillion dollars

C. seven hundred and sixty billion dollars

D. seven hundred and sixty million dollars

30. All of the following constitute the cost of ending child labor EXCEPT _____.

A. building more schools

B. employing more teachers

C. compensating families for the loss of children's income

D. relieving debts for poor countries

PRACTICE TEST 9

PART I DICTATION [15 MIN.]

Listen to the following passage. Altogether the passage will be read to you four times. During the first reading, which will be read at normal speed, listen and try to understand the meaning. For the second and third readings, the passage will be read sentence by sentence, or phrase by phrase, with intervals of 15 seconds. The last reading will be read at normal speed again and during this time you should check your work. You will then be given 2 minutes to check through your work once more.

PART II LISTENING COMPREHENSION [15 MIN.]

In sections A, B and C you will hear everything once only. Listen carefully and then answer the questions that follow.

SECTION A CONVERSATIONS

In this section you will hear several conversations. Listen to the conversations carefully and then answer the questions that follow.

Questions 1 to 3 are based on the following conversation. At the end of the conversation, you will be given 15 seconds to answer the questions.

Now listen to the conversation.

1. What is the woman's attitude toward the man's joining the school football team?
   A. The man should give up.
   B. The man should join by all means.

C. The man should make sure he is healthy enough before joining.

D. It cannot be determined from the conversation.

2. The woman suggested that the man do all of the following EXCEPT _____.

A. have a physical checkup

B. eat healthily

C. strengthen his heart

D. watch TV until midnight

3. The man and the woman are most probably _____.

A. husband and wife

B. colleagues

C. patient and doctor

D. former schoolmates

Questions 4 to 7 are based on the following conversation. At the end of the conversation, you will be given 20 seconds to answer the questions.

Now listen to the conversation.

4. According to Emma, _____.

A. one should start dancing as early as possible

B. the best age for dancing is 19

C. one can dance well even at age 20

D. one can dance well at any age

5. The reason that John wants to take up dancing is that _____.

A. he wants to work out

B. he want to be a professional dancer

C. he want to become an animal trainer

D. he wants to get fun

6. Emma believes that John _____.

A. should dance seriously

B. should learn to be a pro dancer

C. does not know what he dances for

D. cannot dance well

7. What is true of ballet dancers?
   A. They use few muscles
   B. They use lengthy muscles.
   C. They use more muscles than a hockey player.
   D. They develop their muscles very easily.

Questions 8 to 10 are based on the following conversation. At the end of the conversation, you will be given 15 seconds to answer the questions.

Now listen to the conversation.

8. Which of the following is NOT mentioned as symptoms of falling in love?
   A. Exclusive attention to the other person.
   B. Feeling more energetic.
   C. Mentally preoccupied with the other person.
   D. Increased appetite.

9. What is true of romantic love?
   A. It is based on some chemicals.
   B. It is the basis for long-term relationships.
   C. It is closely related to psychology.
   D. It is the opposite of pleasure and excitement.

10. We learn from the conversation that _____.
   A. long-term relationships transcend romantic love
   B. communication forms the foundation for romantic love
   C. romance does harm to long-term relationships
   D. it is impossible to treat your partner as a whole human being

SECTION B   PASSAGES

In this section, you will hear several passages. Listen to the passages carefully and then answer the questions that follow.

Questions 11 *to* 13 *are based on the following passage. At the end of the passage, you will be given* 15 *seconds to answer the questions.*

Now listen to the passage.

11. What is true according to the manager in the World Bank's Development Research Group?
    A. More than 1.3 people around the world live in poverty.
    B. Poverty has reduced dramatically in Africa.
    C. Poverty has dramatically reduced around the world.
    D. Poverty has increased by 20 percent around the world.
12. The Canadian professor believes that _____.
    A. the world Bank's standard for poverty is correct.
    B. poor people should also include those living with more than a dollar a day
    C. living with 14 dollars a day should be regarded as poverty around the world
    D. the poverty around the world has been exaggerated
13. The opinion of the Canadian professor is based on _____.
    A. the economy of the United States
    B. the availability of basic commodities
    C. the increased cost of living in developing countries
    D. the importance of food and fuel

Questions 14 *to* 17 *are based on the following passage. At the end of the passage, you will be given* 20 *seconds to answer the questions.*

Now listen to the passage.

14. Which of the following is NOT true of textbook authors?

A. They present terms and facts professionally.

B. They do not allow for their personal preferences.

C. They let people see things from different perspectives.

D. They present balanced points of views.

15. Which of the following is NOT mentioned as a purpose of writers of newspapers and magazines?

A. To entertain.　　　　　　B. To express personal preferences.

C. To persuade their readers.　D. To yield to readers' views

16. The main purpose of the writers of the editorial pages of newspapers and magazines is to _____.

A. entertain readers

B. express their personal preferences

C. want you to adopt their opinions

D. make you challenge their opinions

17. Writers who intend to persuade you do so by _____.

A. forcing their opinions on you　B. threatening you

C. providing you with reasons　D. dragging you into a debate

Questions 18 *to* 20 *are based on the following passage. At the end of the passage, you will be given* 15 *seconds to answer the questions.*

Now listen to the passage.

18. According to the passage, the gender difference in life expectancy is the greatest _____.

A. in developed countries　　B. among centenarians

C. at birth　　　　　　　　D. in 1500s

19. Women started to live longer than men _____.

A. only in the 1900s

B. only in the 1500s

C. possibly before the 1500s

D. cannot be determined from the passage

20. Which of the following is true?

A. Men suffer more diseases than women.

B. Men suffer more fatal diseases than women.

C. Women do not die as easily from cancer and heart disease as men.

D. Women live longer and enjoy better health than men.

SECTION C   NEWS BROADCAST

Questions 21 and 22 are based on the following news. At the end of the news item, you will be given 10 seconds to answer the questions.

Now listen to the news.

21. The number of people filing for unemployment compensation last week is _____.

A. 30,000   B. 300,000

C. 330,000   D. 360,000

22. The increase in unemployment claims last week _____.

A. is a sign of improved employment situation

B. is surprising

C. is the largest in ten years

D. is less than expected

Questions 23 and 24 are based on the following news. At the end of the news item, you will be given 10 seconds to answer the questions.

Now listen to the news.

23. Which of the following best describes Maradona's condition?

    A. From bad to worse.

    B. Without little sign of improvement.

    C. Improving but still under intense care.

    D. Fully recovered.

24. Maradona's treatment was made difficult by _____.

    A. heart problem   B. drug problem

    C. infection of the lungs   D. rejection of antibiotics

Questions 25 and 26 are based on the following news. At the end of the news item, you will be given 10 seconds to answer the questions.

    Now listen to the news.

25. All of the following are mentioned as alternatives to Western high technology medicine EXCEPT _____.

    A. herbs   B. prayer

    C. deep thinking   D. exercise

26. All of the following words are used similarly EXCEPT _____.

    A. conventional   B. complementary

    C. traditional   D. alternative

Questions 27 and 28 are based on the following news. At the end of the news item, you will be given 10 seconds to answer the questions.

    Now listen to the news.

27. According to the recent finding, the earliest rules for baseball were written in _____.

A. 1791   B. 1839
C. 1869   D. none of these

28. It is possible that the baseball referred to in the Pittsfield law

_____.

A. was played outside the United States
B. was an early version of modern baseball
C. was mostly played by women
D. gave rise to modern cricket

Questions 29 and 30 are based on the following news. At the end of the news item, you will be given 10 seconds to answer the questions.

Now listen to the news.

29. A ban on public smoking will _____.

A. be popular
B. be unpopular
C. dramatically reduce visitors to public places
D. meet strong resistance from smokers

30. Which of the following is true of the government?

A. It feels the pressure to ban public smoking.
B. It has been working hard to ban public smoking.
C. It is not likely to ban public smoking.
D. It will announce a ban on public smoking in March.

PRACTICE TEST 10

PART I DICTATION [15 MIN.]

Listen to the following passage. Altogether the passage will be read to you four times. During the first reading, which will be read at normal speed, listen and try to understand the meaning. For the second and third readings, the passage will be read sentence by sentence, or phrase by phrase, with intervals of 15 seconds. The last reading will be read at normal speed again and during this time you should check your work. You will then be given 2 minutes to check through your work once more.

PART II LISTENING COMPREHENSION [15 MIN.]

In sections A, B and C you will hear everything once only. Listen carefully and then answer the questions that follow.

SECTION A CONVERSATIONS

In this section you will hear several conversations. Listen to the conversations carefully and then answer the questions that follow.

Questions 1 to 3 are based on the following conversation. At the end of the conversation, you will be given 15 seconds to answer the questions.

Now listen to the conversation.

1. Alan implies that at weekends _____.
   A. he seldom watched television
   B. he watched poor television programs
   C. he watched a lot of television

82

D. he watched fewer than 5 hours of television in the evening

2. Alan watched lots of television because _____.

    A. he wanted to relax after working all day

    B. he had problem sleeping

    C. he didn't value his time

    D. the programs were very valuable

3. What is Alan's attitude toward giving up television?

    A. Doubtful.   B. Not serious.

    C. Determined.   D. Tentative.

Questions 4 *to* 7 *are based on the following conversation. At the end of the conversation, you will be given* 20 *seconds to answer the questions.*

    Now listen to the conversation.

4. We learn from the conversation that Tracy _____.

    A. doesn't have enough money for her study

    B. relies solely on her husband's income

    C. may still worry about money

    D. relies solely on her student loan

5. Tracy pays for all of her own education because _____.

    A. she wanted to be independent of her parents

    B. she refused to accept grants

    C. her parents refused to support her

    D. her parents did not have money to support her

6. It seems that Tracy _____ her non-college expenses.

    A. never pays for   B. spends too much money on

    C. is pressured to pay for D. none of these

7. Tracy implies that _____.

    A. expert opinions are not correct

B. students don't have to budget their money

C. college expenses are not very expensive

D. it is difficult for many people to budget their money

Questions 8 to 10 are based on the following conversation. At the end of the conversation, you will be given 15 seconds to answer the questions.

Now listen to the conversation.

8. Which of the following is NOT true?

   A. Cathy dated on the Internet several times.

   B. Cathy talked a lot online with the man before she met him in person.

   C. Cathy was impressed with the man's photo.

   D. Cathy was reluctant to meet the man.

9. Cathy was shocked when she met the man because _____.

   A. she saw the real person

   B. the man had pretended to be someone he was not

   C. she met a wrong man

   D. the man was too intimate toward Cathy

10. What does Cathy think about meeting people in chat rooms?

    A. People are forthcoming with their identities.

    B. There is no risk involved.

    C. It involves too much risk to try.

    D. It is worth trying if handled cautiously.

SECTION B PASSAGES

In this section, you will hear several passages. Listen to the passages carefully and then answer the questions that follow.

Questions 11 to 13 are based on the following passage. At the end of the passage, you will be given 15 seconds to answer the questions.

Now listen to the passage.

11. What is River Bend?
    A. A tourist resort.
    B. A neighborhood community.
    C. A rural sports center.
    D. A neighborhood of 20 to 30 homes.
12. The predominant characteristic of River Bend is _____.
    A. affordability   B. suitability
    C. tranquility   D. individuality
13. All of the following are features of River Bend EXCEPT

    _____.
    A. a sense of identity   B. no care for privacy
    C. little traffic   D. diverse sports facilities

Questions 14 to 17 are based on the following passage. At the end of the passage, you will be given 20 seconds to answer the questions.

Now listen to the passage.

14. What does the new software mainly do?
    A. Help a cell-phone user send photographs.
    B. Organize video conferences for people from around the world.
    C. Recognize a stranger's identity.
    D. Give directions based on received photographs.
15. The difference between the new software and the existing positioning systems lies in _____.
    A. speed   B. accuracy

C. cost D. purpose

16. The new service can do all of the following EXCEPT _____.
    A. tell the direction a customer is facing
    B. match two images of the same building taken differently
    C. inform the customer about a particular building
    D. identify pedestrians and vehicles

17. The commercial future of the service is _____.
    A. unlikely to be bright   B. very bright
    C. bright but short-lived   D. none of these

Questions 18 *to* 20 *are based on the following passage. At the end of the passage, you will be given* 15 *seconds to answer the questions.*

Now listen to the passage.

18. Real bookworms and human bookworms are similar in that
    _____.
    A. they damage the covers of books
    B. their lives are centered around books
    C. they inspire respect in people
    D. they are extremely selfish

19. People tend to think of human bookworms as all of the following
    EXCEPT _____.
    A. passive and lazy   B. controversial
    C. not sociable   D. leading boring lives

20. The author believes that human bookworms _____.
    A. are very choosy about what they read
    B. dislike traveling
    C. feel responsible for the world
    D. have a narrow range of interests

SECTION C   NEWS BROADCAST

Questions 21 and 22 are based on the following news. At the end of the news item, you will be given 10 seconds to answer the questions.

Now listen to the news.

21. The news is mainly about _____.

   A. the consequences of natural disasters in poor countries

   B. the causes of natural disasters in poor countries

   C. different types of natural disasters around the world

   D. how poor countries can reduce the danger of natural disasters

22. The natural disasters in rich and poor countries differ in _____.

   A. intensity   B. frequency

   C. consequence   D. variety

Questions 23 and 24 are based on the following news. At the end of the news item, you will be given 10 seconds to answer the questions.

Now listen to the news.

23. Astronomers are excited that Sedna _____.

   A. is the most distant object in the solar system

   B. consists mainly of ice and dust

   C. is the smallest planet ever found in the solar system

   D. is very much like Pluto and Neptune

24. Which of the following is true of Sedna, according to the news?

   A. It is smaller than a moon.

   B. It is mainly made up of dust.

C. It takes one thousand years for it to orbit the sun.

D. It is about the size of Neptune.

Questions 25 and 26 are based on the following news. At the end of the news item, you will be given 10 seconds to answer the questions.

Now listen to the news.

25. The Senate bill aims to _____ within the next seven years.

    A. end the country's public debts

    B. cut government spendings on health

    C. end the large budget deficit

    D. cut some educational programs

26. Congressional leaders have to work out a compromise because _____.

    A. a similar bill has been passed

    B. the President might oppose the plan

    C. the Senate bill was passed by 57 to 42

    D. the White House is facing opposition

Questions 27 and 28 are based on the following news. At the end of the news item, you will be given 10 seconds to answer the questions.

Now listen to the news.

27. The operation was possible because _____.

    A. they were very young

    B. they were joined at the head

    C. there were not many blood vessels

    D. the two brains were almost separate

28. All of the following are true EXCEPT _____.
   A. the operation went well
   B. the operation was difficult
   C. the boys will have permanent brain damage
   D. it is still unknown if the boys have survived the operation with minimal side effects

Questions 29 and 30 are based on the following news. At the end of the news item, you will be given 10 seconds to answer the questions.

Now listen to the news.

29. Tunisia beat Algeria by a score of _____.
   A. 2:0   B. 4:0   C. 5:3   D. 4:3
30. Which of the following is NOT true of Tunisia?
   A. It has been a strong team.
   B. It claims to be a patriotic country.
   C. It has faced Morocco in several finals.
   D. It has never won the championship of the competition.

第三部分　英语专业四级听力文字材料

TAPESCRIPT OF PRACTICE TEST 1

PART Ⅰ　DICTATION

Listen to the following passage. Altogether the passage will be read to you four times. During the first reading, which will be read at normal speed, listen and try to understand the meaning. For the second and third readings, the passage will be read sentence by sentence, or phrase by phrase, with intervals of 15 seconds. The last reading will be read at normal speed again and during this time you should check your work. You will then be given 2 minutes to check through your work once more.

Now listen to the passage.

CATCHING COLD

There are some steps you can take yourself to avoid catching a cold. / Contrary to popular belief, colds are not caused by exposure to severe weather. / Colds are caused by viruses harbored in the body, / and you're better off out on the ski slopes/ than you are in room surrounded by people/ who just may be passing the virus around. / If you feel a chill, you're already a sick. / A chill is an early symptom: / It's the cold that caused the chill, not the other way around. /

While the virus can spread when a cold-sufferer coughs or sneezes, / this is not the most common route of transmission. / The overwhelming majority of colds are caught by hand contact. / A cold-sufferer rubs her nose, / thereby transferring the virus to her hand. / Then a friend comes to visit and presses her hand. /

The second and third readings. You should begin writing now.
The last reading. Now, you have two minutes to check through your work.

PART Ⅱ   LISTENING COMPREHENSION

In sections A, B and C you will hear everything once only. Listen carefully and then answer the questions that follow.

SECTION A   CONVERSATIONS

In this section you will hear several conversations. Listen to the conversations carefully and then answer the questions that follow.

Questions 1 to 3 are based on the following conversation. At the end of the conversation, you will be given 15 seconds to answer the questions.

Now listen to the conversation.

Billy: Sally, how are you doing?

Sally: I'm doing fine. I've spent the last two years studying Chinese literature on the lovely Chinese coast. I could not have made a better choice, as I really enjoy everything about being here except the lack of snow, of course!

Billy: Why did you choose to study Chinese literature?

Sally: Well, my parents are China scholars, and since I was very young I've been interested in China, especially Chinese culture. I have always believed that a country's literature reveals a lot about its culture.

Billy: What do you like about your study?

Sally: What I like most is that we have group work, presentations and assignments as well as seminars and lectures. These variations enable interaction and discussion among the students.

Billy: Say something more about the place of your study, will you?

Sally: It's a great student town because of its size and nightlife. You will not experience being lost or lonely here. Unfortunately for some, there is a lack of opportunities for those interested in art.

Billy: I guess it's still a wonderful place.

Sally: It sure is. It can offer friendly people, a gorgeous beach, powerful waves and a fresh sea breeze. Nothing else can refresh you more than a walk by the beach!

Questions 4 *to* 6 *are based on the following conversation. At the end of the conversation, you will be given* 15 *seconds to answer the questions.*

Now listen to the conversation.

Warren: Henry, did you watch the BASE jump, I mean, fifteen people jumped from the tallest building with parachutes yesterday?

Henry: No. It must have been exciting to watch it?

Warren: You bet. It seems to me they hit the ground in a split second, though it actually took them longer than that.

Henry: They must have opened their parachutes pretty late.

Warren: Yes. Without parachutes it would take them eight seconds to hit the ground. Actually, they opened their parachutes with a few seconds' delay.

Henry: Wow. If I had had to jump, I would have opened my parachute immediately upon jumping.

Warren: These were professional BASE jumpers. But in BASE jumping the margins of error are small because BASE jumpers don't have as much freefall as skydivers and therefore don't have as much time to make adjustment or correct errors.

Henry: So it must be a dangerous sport.

Warren: Yes. Also, BASE jumping is performed near solid objects such as cliffs and dams, so any error can cause serious injury or death.

Henry: Is BASE jumping as popular as skydiving?

Warren: Not quite. But contrary to popular belief, there is a wide section of society that enjoy this sport of freedom and excitement.

Questions 7 to 10 are based on the following conversation. At the end of the conversation, you will be given 15 seconds to answer the questions.

Now listen to the conversation.

Lisa: Frank, are you happy? I mean you have a big house and you have a car.

Frank: I don't know, Lisa. A lot of people also have houses and cars.

Lisa: You mean you want to have more than other people and this will make you happy?

Frank: Possibly.

Lisa: Then you're looking for relative happiness.

Frank: Ok, Lisa, what do you think is happiness?

Lisa: Well, through the centuries, people have offered quite different definitions of happiness such as: happy people were married women and single men, or happiness meant self-gratification, or happiness could be achieved by eating less or eating more.

Frank: So happiness is rather elusive?

Lisa: I think the happiest people are those who find joy in their daily lives, and who enjoy their friendships, families, work and hobbies.

Frank: You mean they are not bothered by the desire to get something more, something new, something better?

Lisa: You couldn't be more correct. One more thing, Frank. If you are happy, you may not be satisfied with your life.

Frank: What do you mean?

Lisa: Happiness often means how happy you feel with your life now. Satisfaction often means that people have to take a step back from their lives and look at them in general.

SECTION B   PASSAGES

In this section, you will hear several passages. Listen to the passages carefully and then answer the questions that follow.

Questions 11 to 13 are based on the following passage. At the end of the passage, you will be given 15 seconds to answer the questions.

Now listen to the passage.

When discussing food and diet, it is always necessary to treat the world's population as two separate groups: those who have more food than they really need and those who suffer shortages of even the most basic foods. People in developed countries have such a wide variety of foods to choose from that sometimes making a choice can be

94

a bit of a problem. For many in the developing countries, the problem is not what to eat but if they have anything to eat at all. But those who face the problem of having little or nothing to eat are just the tip of the iceberg. For each one of these, there are many more who are suffering from the effects of malnutrition. They have food, but not enough and usually of a wrong sort. They may have just enough to keep them alive but because it doesn't have the nutrients necessary to keep them healthy, they get sick very easily and usually die young.

We may think the problem is caused by the simple fact that there are two many people or there is not enough food in the world. But according to a World Bank report, we have enough food. The real problem lies not so much in a shortage of food as in the ability of the poor people to buy or grow enough food to keep them healthy.

Questions 14 *to* 17 *are based on the following passage. At the end of the passage, you will be given* 20 *seconds to answer the questions.*

Now listen to the passage.

Employers spend thousands of dollars and countless hours on training and continuing education, all with hopes of improving productivity and boosting employee spirit. But all too often, they fail to spend time and money on providing a workplace setting where employees can best use their skills. But many of us go to work every day and enter our workspace without even thinking twice about the surroundings and how they affect us. We come to work and do our jobs without thinking about how an improved setting could improve productivity.

It's safe to say there's no corporate standard when it comes to designing the workplace. What works for one company might not work for another company or department. And the debate about whether to go with an open office environment versus a private office culture will go on forever. But no matter what the latest and greatest trends are, the corporate cubicle setting will somehow always be a part of the workplace. However, it doesn't have to be the traditional setting, with three walls dividing you from the rest of the group and a desk and trays to store paper, family photos, and old office memos. According to a 2002 survey, 10 percent of offices are completely barrier-free with no partitions separating workstations. In these settings, everyone—even management and executives—sits in the open.

Questions 18 to 20 are based on the following passage. At the end of the passage, you will be given 15 seconds to answer the questions.

Now listen to the passage.

It is generally believed that humans began to control fire 250,000 years ago. Now scientists in Israel have found signs of controlled burning more than three times that old.

The evidence that the fire was controlled rather than natural is strong. The scientists found the burned wood in clusters, suggesting locations where people had used fires regularly. If a natural fire had had occurred, the distribution of burnt items would have been irregular, to be spread all over the site.

What the scientists have to do now is to find examples of the earliest use of fire in Europe. There is evidence of early human settlements in England about 500,000 years ago, but no signs of any man-made fires there. Until now, European archaeologists have not concentrated enough on this topic, so it is about time they started looking harder for this kind of evidence, but if humans did not have fire and yet they colonized these fairly cold countries, then it means that humans were more adaptable than we thought they were.

SECTION C   NEWS BROADCAST

Questions 21 *and* 22 *are based on the following news. At the end of the news item, you will be given* 10 *seconds to answer the questions.*

Now listen to the news.

The World Health Organization has expressed concern that bird flu has for the first time broken out in a number of Asian countries simultaneously. A WHO official told BBC that the unprecedented scale of the outbreak could make it difficult to rein in(控制)the virus. Cases of bird flu have been detected in Japan, Taiwan of China, South Korea as well as in Vietnam where five people died after they caught the disease. Tests are now being carried out in Thailand to see whether the disease is present.

Questions 23 *and* 24 *are based on the following news. At the end of the news item, you will be given* 10 *seconds to answer the questions.*

Now listen to the news.

The United States Supreme Court says it will consider whether it's constitutional to execute people who are under the age of 18 when they commit their crimes.

Eleven years ago in the mid-western state of Missouri a young male, aged 17, robbed a woman and threw her off a bridge. He was convicted（被判有罪）and sentenced to death. But a high court in Missouri decided that his execution would be unconstitutional because he was so young. That case has now made its way to the US Supreme Court. The Court's nine justices will decide whether the execution should go ahead, and in doing so they will decide whether it's legal for some American states to execute those under 18 when they offend.

Question 25 is based on the following news. At the end of the news item, you will be given 5 seconds to answer the question.
Now listen to the news.

Relief workers in Iran say they're concentrating on the immediate needs of tens of thousands of people left homeless by Friday's earthquake. Rescue teams have spent a third day searching for bodies in the rubble in the city of Bam, but they believe it's unlikely more people will be found alive. The Iranian government now puts the number of dead at more than twenty-two thousand.

So far much of the immediate effort has been focused on trying to save people who might still be alive and trapped under the rubble（废墟）. But now there's a consensus（一致意见）that no more search and rescue teams are needed. There are hundreds of rescue experts here sent by 26 different nations, along with specialist equipment and sniffer dogs（嗅犬）. But there is little success now in terms of finding live survivors, and the search and rescue operation is expected to be called off.

Questions 26 to 28 are based on the following news. At the end of the news item, you will be given 15 seconds to answer the questions.

Now listen to the news.

An international conference opens in London today to try to find new ways of tackling poverty in Asia where two thirds of the world's poor people live. Despite the success of such economies as Japan and South Korea and impressive growth in China and India, more than a billion Asians live on less than a dollar a day. The conference is an attempt to put spotlight on Asia after years in which much of the focus has been on Africa. Even within those booming economies, many people are excluded, creating great wealth gaps between rural and urban areas, men and women, and different ethnic groups. So one of the biggest questions now is how to manage Asia's growth in a more stable and inclusive way.

Questions 29 and 30 are based on the following news. At the end of the news item, you will be given 10 seconds to answer the questions.

Now listen to the news.

Hong Kong's Hang Seng index continued its rise this week after a short-lived correction in early February. The main share index was up more than three percent for the week, closing Friday at 13,739.

Taiwan's Taiex reached a fresh 40-month high on Friday. It gained three percent for the week, ending at 6,549. Traders said the strong performance in property shares drove the gains in financial stocks. Traditionally, banks and other lenders benefit when there is enthusiasm for real estate.

Tokyo's Nikkei index also closed higher Friday, adding about one percent for the week to finish Friday at 10,557. Japanese real estate and banking shares were generally trading higher.

South Korean investors turned their attention to strong earnings results from some market leaders this week. Seoul's Kospi index ended the week 3. 7 percent higher at 882.

TAPESCRIPT OF PRACTICE TEST 2

PART I DICTATION

Listen to the following passage. Altogether the passage will be read to you four times. During the first reading, which will be read at normal speed, listen and try to understand the meaning. For the second and third readings, the passage will be read sentence by sentence, or phrase by phrase, with intervals of 15 seconds. The last reading will be read at normal speed again and during this time you should check your work. You will then be given 2 minutes to check through your work once more.

Now listen to the passage.

BICYLCLES OR CARS

Thirty years ago, the bicycle was the king of China's city streets. / Rivers of bike riders streamed through every city and town, / and a bicycle was one of the most desired wedding presents a couple could receive. / Today, a shiny new car is the choice. /

Shanghai is a city of almost 10 million bicycles. / Because of China's new love affair with the motor vehicle, / bike riders are being edged off the crowded streets.

Last December, Shanghai officials announced a plan/ that would prevent cyclists from riding on many of the city's major routes. / Angry letters to newspapers followed. / In February, the government bowed to public displeasure, / and promised to build a network of paths for cyclists throughout the city. /

But it is still tough for cyclists in Shanghai, / as they fight for space with aggressive motorists, / many of whom have only just obtained their licenses. /

The second and third readings. You should begin writing now.
The last reading. Now, you have two minutes to check through
your work.

PART Ⅱ   LISTENING COMPREHENSION

In sections A, B and C you will hear everything once only.
Listen carefully and then answer the questions that follow.

SECTION A   CONVERSATIONS

In this section you will hear several conversations. Listen to the
conversations carefully and then answer the questions that follow.

Questions 1 to 3 are based on the following conversation. At the
end of the conversation, you will be given 15 seconds to answer the
questions.

Now listen to the conversation.

Jassie: Hello, Jeff.

Jeff: Hello, Jassie.

Jassie: Do you know that Argentina's former football player
        Maradona is back in the news?

Jeff: What's happened?

Jassie: He's been hospitalized for heart and respiratory problems.

Jeff: Is it serious?

Jassie: Well, he's on a respirator and in intensive care.

Jeff: I hope he'll get well. Anyway, Maradona is a football
        legend. He's ranked among such names as Michael Jordan,
        Muhammad Ali, and Pele.

Jassie: I don't know. At least others don't abuse drugs.

Jeff: Don't you know he's just a human being?

Jassie: People often held, and still hold, him as a role model, but he seems to have let us down.

Jeff: It all depends on how you look at it. Aren't you impressed with his talents? Do you still remember his finest moment when he danced through the defense of England to score possibly the greatest individual goal in the history of the sport back in 1986?

Jassie: That moment cannot be exaggerated(这一时刻再怎么夸张也不过分), but what makes a great athlete is more than his or her professional skills.

Jeff: You may have a point there, but...

Jassie: He's also blamed for scandal, corruption and weird behaviors.

Jeff: Well, you seem to have a strong case, but, as they say, no man is perfect.

Questions 4 to 7 are based on the following conversation. At the end of the conversation, you will be given 20 seconds to answer the questions.

Now listen to the conversation.

Peter: My brother Mike has just done a course at the Green Park Camping School.

Linda: Really! What made him decide to do that?

Peter: Well, for one thing, some boys in his class decided to do it and they dared him to go with them!

Linda: You mean he didn't really want to go?

Peter: I think he wanted to go but I think he was also a little frightened. Of course, now that he's done it, he's very

103

pleased with himself and he's always talking about it.

Linda: So he enjoyed it, didn't he?

Peter: Not exactly. I think he's enjoying the feeling of having done it more than he enjoyed actually doing it!

Linda: What sort of things did he do?

Peter: Oh, all sorts of open-air activities: hiking, camping, canoeing (划小木舟). One thing he had to do was to capsize a canoe and then right it again without getting out. He said the water was very cold but that he hardly noticed it at the time.

Linda: Why not?

Peter: He was too busy righting the canoe!

Linda: That doesn't sound very comfortable at this time of they year.

Peter: That's what he said when he told me. On another occasion he had to spend a day and a night by himself in the open country.

Linda: Was he frightened?

Peter: He was at first, apparently, but then he got used to it.

Linda: It seems to me that the course did him a lot of good. I expect it's made him more self-reliant.

Peter: That's what he says—and now he wants me to go!

Questions 8 to 10 are based on the following conversation. At the end of the conversation, you will be given 15 seconds to answer the questions.

Now listen to the conversation.

Cathy: Frank, which do you prefer, city or country life?

Frank: It's a fifty-fifty choice and it largely depends on the individual. But the bottom line is that each life has its own advantages and disadvantages.

104

Cathy: You're right there. Generally speaking, people in the city are better paid And according to the latest study, the income disparity between the city and the country is three to one. Isn't that alarming!

Frank: But living in the country is less expensive, although the costs of transportation are much higher.

Cathy: I think that philosophy is the root of the difference. In the city, people want to "do it all in one day." In the country, people don't expect to get it all done in one day. Country folks tend to plan more because planning is required just to survive.

Frank: In the country, you mind your own business without being unfriendly or unneighborly. And there are a lot less restrictions on what you can do, whether or not there is a law about it. Many laws on the books are not enforced.

Cathy: Also, there is no real crime to speak of. Any petty crime is usually committed by the local school kids and is nothing serious. Every murder I can think of was a result of domestic violence, so in the country you are in more danger from your family than you are a stranger.

Frank: But the city continues to attract people from the country, rather than the other way around.

SECTION B PASSAGES

In this section, you will hear several passages. Listen to the passages carefully and then answer the questions that follow.

Questions 11 to 13 are based on the following passage. At the end of the passage, you will be given 15 seconds to answer the questions.

Now listen to the passage.

A national political struggle is continuing over the issue of protection for the remains of vast ancient forests that once covered the northwestern areas of the United States. These old forests, called "old growth," contain trees from 200 to 1,200 years old. There are now about 6 million acres of virgin forest in Washington and Oregon, only about one-tenth of what existed before the 1800's. This old growth contains some of the valuable timber in the nation, but its economic worth is also contained in its water, wildlife, scenery, and recreational facilities.

Conservationists want the majority of existing old growth protected from harvesting. They emphasize the vital relationship between old growth and the health of the forest's ecosystem. They quote studies that show that both downed and standing old trees store and release nutrients necessary to young trees.

On the other hand, much of the Northwest's economy is developed around the timber industry. Trees are cut down to make wood products, and many mills are equipped for old growth industry. In recent years, 500 acres of old growth have been cut, including some trees up to 500 years old and eight feet in diameter. Although the U. S. Forest Service is considering the problem of how much of the forest to save, the harvesting of timber continues. The district office refuses to remove any of the old growth from timber production. The struggle is continuing at the national level, with strong supporters on both sides.

Questions 14 to 17 are based on the following passage. At the end of the passage, you will be given 20 seconds to answer the questions.

Now listen to the passage.

The most useful sort of exercise is exercise that develops the heart, lungs, and circulatory systems. If these systems are fit, the body is ready for almost any sport and for almost any sudden demand by work or emergencies. One can train more specifically to develop strength for weight lifting or to develop the ability to run straight ahead for short distances with great power as in football, but running trains your heart and lungs to deliver oxygen more efficiently to all parts of your body.

Only one sort of equipment is needed, that is, a good pair of shoes. Many design advances have been made that make an excellent running shoe indispensable if a runner wishes to develop as quickly as possible, with as little chance of injury as possible. A good running shoe will have a soft pad for absorbing shock, as well as a slightly built-up heel and a full heel cup that will give the knee and ankle more stability. A wise investment in good shoes will prevent blisters(水泡) and foot, ankle, and knee injuries and will also enable the wearer to run on paved or soft surfaces.

No other special equipment is needed; you can jog in any clothing you desire, even your street clothes. Many joggers wear expensive, flashy warm-up suits, but just as many wear a simple pair of gym shorts and T-shirts. In cold weather, several layers of clothing are better than one heavy sweater or coat. If joggers are wearing several layers of clothing, they can add or reduce layers as conditions change.

Questions 18 *to* 20 *are based on the following passage. At the end of the passage, you will be given* 15 *seconds to answer the questions.*

Now listen to the passage.

Advertising offers some great advantages to consumers. For example, in order to keep prices low through mass production, companies must have a mass market for their products. Mass advertising creates mass markets. Producers cannot afford to develop new products and wait for the customers to discover them. This would take too long. Demand for some products must be created. This is done through advertising.

But advertising sometimes makes it difficult for customers to make wise decisions. The fact is that when people are constantly flooded with messages through mass media, persuading them to buy particular products, many respond by buying them.

Advertising is designed to influence an individual to buy a product. Sellers often study human behavior to discover what will convince consumers to buy a certain item. This reason for buying is called a buying motive.

Buying motives are usually broken down into two categories: rational and emotional. Rational buying motives include the desire to save money, the desire for comfort, or the desire for good quality. Emotional buying motives include buying out of fear, wanting to feel good, or wanting to have something better than your friends have.

Most customers believe that they are not easily influenced by emotional appeals. However, corporations that sell consumer products obviously think differently. They spend many millions of dollars every day on radio, television, newspaper and magazine ads that use these appeals.

SECTION C   NEWS BROADCAST

Questions 21 *and* 22 *are based on the following news. At the end of the news item, you will be given* 10 *seconds to answer the questions.*

Now listen to the news.

About 100 people are now known to have died in what have been described as the worse storms ever to hit the eastern US this century. The hurricane-force winds first struck the Gulf of Mexico, and have now spread across the Canadian border, continuing to bring record snowfalls, sever flooding and causing millions of dollars of damage. All major airports have now reopened and airlines are beginning to cope with the backlog of thousands of stranded passengers. The storms also paralyzed areas of Cuba where several people were killed and property and crops destroyed.

Questions 23 and 24 are based on the following news. At the end of the news item, you will be given 10 seconds to answer the questions.
Now listen to the news.

Israeli Prime Minister Sharon is in stable condition after undergoing five hours of emergency surgery to reduce pressure in his brain and stop new breeding. Following surgery the 77 year old underwent a cat scan and doctors say there have been significant improvement from when he arrived at the hospital Thursday evening. However he does remain in critical condition.

Questions 25 and 26 are based on the following news. At the end of the news item, you will be given 10 seconds to answer the question.
Now listen to the news.

Scientists in the United States have taken the first step towards developing a drug to treat the SARS respiratory disease which killed nearly 800 people last year. They've developed a human antibody that can bind to the SARS virus and stop it from invading human cells in the test tube. The research published in the Proceedings of National Academy of Sciences could also lead to a preventive vaccine for the disease, although most experts agree this could take years.

Questions 27 and 28 are based on the following news. At the end of the news item, you will be given 10 seconds to answer the questions.

Now listen to the news.

The head of the investigation into the January 3 crash of a chartered Egyptian airliner off the Egyptian coast said Tuesday there is no possibility that an explosion caused the Boeing 737 to crash into the Red Sea. Lead investigator Shaker Qilada said he could confirm that the crash was not the result of a terrorist act. He said the crash was definitely caused by a technical problem that could include mechanical failure or pilot error. Investigators said while the aircraft's flight data recorder indicated there was no explosion, initial analysis of the voice cockpit recorder which contains pilot conversations did not explain what went wrong with the jetliner.

Questions 29 and 30 are based on the following news. At the end of the news item, you will be given 10 seconds to answer the questions.

Now listen to the news.

Two gunmen have attacked an office of the UN refugee agency in southern Sudan, killing a local guard and wounding two workers.

The UNHCR said it was still seeking more details about the attack in the southern town of Yei. The two wounded UNHCR employees are being treated in hospital in the southern capital, Juba, before being airlifted in Nairobi, Kenya. Following the attack, the planned return of refugees in Democratic Republic of Congo has been suspended.

TAPESCRIPT OF PRACTICE TEST 3

PART I   DICTATION

Listen to the following passage. Altogether the passage will be read to you four times. During the first reading, which will be read at normal speed, listen and try to understand the meaning. For the second and third readings, the passage will be read sentence by sentence, or phrase by phrase, with intervals of 15 seconds. The last reading will be read at normal speed again and during this time you should check your work. You will then be given 2 minutes to check through your work once more.

Now listen to the passage.

ANTI-SMOKING CAMPAIGN MADE DIFFICULT

There is more to be done than telling people why they should stop smoking, / if a national campaign is to be truly successful. / The health reasons for not smoking are obvious. / But generally they do not discourage cigarette abuse. / Young smokers, for example, are not particularly frightened by threats of major illnesses/ that may not strike for thirty or forty years. / They may be influenced more by findings about harmed breathing. / Every phase of lung function is impaired/ when cigarette smokers and non-smokers are compared. / The airways are narrower and gas transfer is reduced, / so that less oxygen gets to the blood and body tissues. /

There are many forces that make the quick elimination of cigarette smoking unlikely. / The farm families who produce the 2 billion pounds of tobacco / experience lung cancer at the same

112

increasing rate as the rest of the population,/ but will statistics convince them that they should change their occupation? /

The second and third readings. You should begin writing now.

The last reading. Now, you have two minutes to check through your work.

PART Ⅱ LISTENING COMPREHENSION

In sections A, B and C you will hear everything once only. Listen carefully and then answer the questions that follow.

SECTION A CONVERSATIONS

In this section you will hear several conversations. Listen to the conversations carefully and then answer the questions that follow.

Questions 1 to 4 are based on the following conversation. At the end of the conversation, you will be given 20 seconds to answer the questions.

Now listen to the conversation.

Rebecca: Berry, you're just back from Rio de Janeiro?
Berry: Yeah.
Rebecca: What was it like?
Berry: Well, the first two days in Rio was quite a shock for us. Here it was a lot of fat middle-aged Europeans and Americans exercising along the beach, sunbathing, walking with their walkmans. It's a big contrast to the thousands of people sleeping on the street during night.
Rebecca: What was the weather like?
Berry: The climate is very different from other places such as Peru or Bolivia. We were at sea level, and we all felt very good

113

about it. No one of us needed to breathe extra air from time to time, and the temperature is about 25 degrees and the air is very humid.

Rebecca: That's really nice.

Berry: The first day we had very nice weather, and were able to really relax on the beach. After these two days we had bad weather, rain and cloudy. So, we're a little bit disappointed about that. Due to the weather, we explored the old part of Rio.

Rebecca: How about the food there?

Berry: We ate at local restaurant. This restaurant has a fixed fee of about ten US dollars. Then you can eat as much as you want from a vast and delicate buffet(自助餐)consisting of both seafood and meat. Desert and drinks are not included.

Rebecca: It's been really a nice trip.

Berry: Well, Rio was not the experience we had hoped for, and we feel that this city is over-publicized. But anyway it's cool to have been there.

Questions 5 to 7 are based on the following conversation. At the end of the conversation, you will be given 15 seconds to answer the questions.

Now listen to the conversation.

Jim: Hi, Victoria. Which year of college are you in now?

Victoria: I'm in my third and final year. I am reading law and am determined to get a decent degree by the end of this year! I will therefore be studying a lot more than I did last year!

Jim: How do you like being a student?

Victoria: Being a student is great. Coming to university and living

114

away from parents is the best social thing you'll ever do. I've made lots of friends and there is always someone to go downtown with.

Jim: I guess you are living on campus as many students do?

Victoria: I lived in student halls in the first two years. I am now living off campus with my aunt and uncle, because I will get much more work done with fewer distractions! Plus my friends can't come and drag me out every night!

Jim: How about your studies?

Victoria: This semester I am studying three subjects, two of them my own choice. I have no coursework so I have to try and keep on top of my work so I can prepare for my exams rather than learn the material for the first time and cram.

Jim: Do you study your subjects on your own since you have no coursework?

Victoria: Every student has a personal tutor, and mine is wonderful! He's helped me out a number of times from motivating me when I was ready to quit, to explaining things in a different way to help me obtain a better mark. Basically your personal tutor will help you with anything, and most of the lectures are helpful anyway. Just yesterday my lecturer gave me four of his own books to keep so I could read them at home, which saved me a fortune.

Questions 8 to 10 are based on the following conversation. At the end of the conversation, you will be given 15 seconds to answer the questions.

Now listen to the conversation.

Jane: Kerry, do you agree that newspapers seem impersonal?

Kerry: Yes. There're no personalities involved as in radio or TV.

Jane: Yes. But being impersonal does not mean objectivity. Newspapers are written by people who have biases and prejudices.

Kerry: You said it(你说得对). On the other hand, radio and television can be just as biased as, if not more biased than, newspapers.

Jane: The difference between newspapers on the one hand and radio and television on the other is personality.

Kerry: Yes. When you read a newspaper article, it's kind of cold.

Jane: There're no voice inflections.

Kerry: And there're no facial expressions or body language, either.

Jane: It could be a real exciting story, and all you can do is put exclamation marks.

Kerry: But on camera, people can interpret the words of a script in their voices and expressions.

Jane: That would have an impact on the audience.

Kerry: Yes. People are more likely to influenced by what's offered on radio and television than in newspapers.

Jane: Of course, newspaper writers can use descriptive words such as adjectives or adverbs, but that's nothing compared with personalities.

Kerry: Yes.

Jane: Personality sells.

SECTION B   PASSAGES

In this section, you will hear several passages. Listen to the passages carefully and then answer the questions that follow.

Questions 11 to 13 are based on the following passage. At the end of the passage, you will be given 15 seconds to answer the

116

questions.

Now listen to the passage.

A balanced diet contains proteins, which are composed of complex amino acids(氨基酸). There are 20 types of amino acids, comprising about 16 percent of the body weight in an individual. A body needs all 20 to be healthy. Amino acids can be divided into two groups: essential and nonessential. There are nine essential amino acids. These are the proteins that the body cannot produce by itself, so a healthy individual must get them through food. The 11 nonessential amino acids, on the other hand, are produced by the body, so it is not necessary to get them through food. Proteins are described as being either high-quality or low-quality. This refers to how many of the nine essential amino acids the food contains. High-quality proteins, typically found in animal meats, are proteins which have sufficient amounts of the essential amino acids. Low-quality proteins are mainly plant proteins and usually lack one or more essential amino acids. Since people who follow a strict vegetarian diet are only eating food of low-quality proteins, they must make sure that their diets contain a variety of proteins, in order to insure that what is lacking in one food is available in another. The process of selecting a variety of the essential proteins is called protein complementation. Since an insufficient amount of protein in the diet can be harmful to a person's health, and prolonged absence of proteins can cause death, it is imperative that a vegetarian diet contains an ample amount of the essential proteins.

Questions 14 to 17 are based on the following passage. At the end of the passage, you will be given 20 seconds to answer the questions.

Now listen to the passage.

Hong Kong, the Netherlands, and Britain are among the best places to do business, according to a new survey. More and more countries have been developing a financial infrastructure as a key to their economic development over the past year.

There is more good news from Asian countries that suffered in the financial crisis of the late 1990s. They have, for the most part, started to deal with some of the problems in their financial system and to improve their ability to convert savings to investment.

Asia's financial giant, China, is one of the countries making improvements. The United States has diversified capital markets, but most Chinese businesses get their financing from banks. The banks in China provide about 80 percent of the financing to generate the growth that's occurred over the years. What China needs now is to broaden its capital markets.

Other countries such as Romania, Pakistan, Croatia and most of Africa have fallen behind. There are a number of reasons such as the lack of concentration of economic and political power. Those are also countries that have less democratic systems for the most part, and those are the countries that have suffered the most from the absence of more developed financial systems.

The United States fell from third to sixth place in the survey of capital markets because of corporate scandals and concerns about transparency.

Questions 18 to 20 are based on the following passage. At the end of the passage, you will be given 15 seconds to answer the questions.

Now listen to the passage.

Love can be seen everywhere. Yet surprisingly, love has been the subject of less scientific research than other emotions, such as anger and fear. The reason for this is twofold. First, love is a very complex emotion, difficult to describe and measure. Secondly, unlike many extreme emotions, extreme love is generally not a problem; thus less medical attention has been paid to it.

Love is an enduring, strong, positive attraction and feeling for another person or thing. But it is more than this. It also involves feelings of caring, protection, excitement, and tenderness. Sometimes it is easier to think in terms of different kinds of love: "puppy" love, romantic love, brotherly love, and so froth. Though they differ in some respects, they share one important characteristic: a strong positive feeling toward another.

Our feelings toward other people are often complex. We may love someone and, at the same time, be angry with him. Or we may love someone, even though we are jealous of him. We might love someone and, at the same time, hate for specific reasons.

Hate is a strong negative emotion toward someone, and is due to anger, jealousy, or some other factor. Like love, hate can be a very strong emotion. The questions is often asked, " Is it bad to hate?" Usually hate does not help us; it makes us feel unhappy and makes us do things that may hurt others. However, sometimes it may be necessary to hate and hurt someone in order to protect loved ones.

SECTION C   NEWS BROADCAST

Questions 21 *and* 22 *are based on the following news. At the end of the news item, you will be given* 10 *seconds to answer the questions.*

Now listen to the news.

When Nobel Peace laureate(获奖者)Shirin Ebadi returned to Iran after receiving the prize, tens of thousands of Iranians took to the streets to cheer her. Ms. Ebadi was born, raised and educated in Iran. Before the revolution she was one of the first female judges in the country. Now she works as a lawyer and teaches at Tehran University. The Nobel Committee, in awarding Ms. Ebadi the prize, noted that although she's been imprisoned for her work on several controversial political cases, she's worked persistently for women's rights, children's rights and human rights, and has also promoted the interpretation of the Islamic law that is agreeable with democracy.

Questions 23 to 25 are based on the following news. At the end of the news item, you will be given 15 seconds to answer the questions.

Now listen to the news.

United States government has approved a drug that aims to treat cancer in an entirely new way. The drug known as Avastin works by starving cancerous tumors of blood, thus preventing them from growing. Clinical trials have show Avastin to prolong the lives of those with advanced colon cancer by about five months.

This has been seen as a potentially very significant breakthrough in the fight against cancer. The drug has been shown to prevent the formation of new blood vessels, thereby denying tumors the oxygen and other nutrients needed for their growth. The company that created the drug says it is now looking at how Avastin might be used to treat other common cancers such as breast cancer and lung cancer. Unlike chemotherapy(化疗), which works by killing all dividing cells

120

in the body and therefore has serious side effects, the potential benefit of this new approach is that the drug would only target the tumors themselves.

Questions 26 and 27 are based on the following news. At the end of the news item, you will be given 10 seconds to answer the question.

Now listen to the news.

A major shareholder protest has forced the entertainment giant Walt Disney to make radical changes in the way the company is led. Disney's top manager Michael Eisner lost his position as chairman of the board after 43% of shareholders withheld(拒绝给予)their support from him.

The Disney board has surrendered to the great force of shareholders' discontent. One of the big criticisms had been that Michael Eisner had too much power as both chairman and chief executive of the company. Accordingly the job will now be split. He'll continue in the main executive role, but George Mitchell, who negotiated peace in Northern Island, will take over as chairman. The shareholders said that such a solution would not be acceptable. Mr. Mitchell has been too closely involved with the existing Disney policy for them to be satisfied.

Questions 28 and 29 are based on the following news. At the end of the news item, you will be given 10 seconds to answer the questions.

Now listen to the news.

A team of researchers at the Massachusetts Institute of

Technology, Boston, US, are working on a new technology in the digital world. In the future, you could feel somebody shake your hand when they call you over on their mobile phone. You could be talking to somebody over a mobile phone and you could squeeze the phone and they would feel some sense of that squeeze at the other end. The research is still in its early stages, but the team is enthusiastic about the possibilities for the new technology.

Question 30 is based on the following news. At the end of the news item, you will be given 5 seconds to answer the questions.
Now listen to the news.

International scientists say that they believe the human outbreaks of the Ebola virus in central Africa was started when hunters handled dead bodies of infected wild animals. In a report to be published in Friday's issue of the US journal of Science, researchers say animal epidemics often precede human ones, and it might be possible to predict and prevent human outbreaks by setting up networks to monitor Ebola deaths among wild life.

TAPESCRIPT OF PRACTICE TEST 4

PART I DICTATION

Listen to the following passage. Altogether the passage will be read to you four times. During the first reading, which will be read at normal speed, listen and try to understand the meaning. For the second and third readings, the passage will be read sentence by sentence, or phrase by phrase, with intervals of 15 seconds. The last reading will be read at normal speed again and during this time you should check your work. You will then be given 2 minutes to check through your work once more.

Now listen to the passage.

HOME - HEART OF FAMILY

Looking back on years of living in working-class home in the North of England,/ I should say that a good living-room provide three principle things:/ sociability, warmth and plenty of good food. / The living-room is the warm heart of the family/ and therefore often slightly stuffy to a middle-class visitor. / It is not a social center but a family center:/ little entertaining goes on there or in the front room. / The wife's social life outside her immediate family/ is found over the washing-line or visiting relatives. / The husband visits his pub or club,/ and he also has his work and his football matches. / The couple have friends at all these places,/ who may well not know what the inside of their house is like. / The family hearth is reserved for the family itself. / Much of their free time will usually be passed at that heart. /

The second and third readings. You should begin writing now.
The last reading. Now, you have two minutes to check through
your work.

PART II LISTENING COMPREHENSION

In sections A, B and C you will hear everything once only.
Listen carefully and then answer the questions that follow.

SECTION A CONVERSATIONS

In this section you will hear several conversations. Listen to the
conversations carefully and then answer the questions that follow.

Questions 1 to 3 are based on the following conversation. At the
end of the conversation, you will be given 15 seconds to answer the
questions.

Now listen to the conversation.

Professor Walter: Miss Lauren, why don't you attend class
discussions? Is it because you feel shy speaking?

Miss Lauren: Well, although I prefer quiet and independent study, I
do believe participation in class discussions facilitates
good understanding of learning materials. The
problems is that the topics are too difficult, there's a
lack of planning for some of the topics, and someone
seems to dominate the conversation all the time.

Professor Walter: Maybe we should improve our discussions, but
when someone dominates, you should assert yourself
and speak up.

Miss Lauren: Maybe I should speak more. But there are some
students in class who I think are very smart but who
don't speak up either. We don't want to hurt

someone's feelings.

Professor Walter: In class discussions there's equal chance of speaking, so there's no need for too much politeness or sensitivity.

Miss Lauren: But I hope some other students should also speak more. They seem to be intimidated to speak up in class.

Professor Walter: I think they should. Also, as much as I appreciate your independent study, you should get to know other students well so that you will feel like participating in discussions among friends rather than strangers.

Miss Lauren: I will do as you say. On the other hand, you should prepare questions that ask students to describe their own experiences as they relate to a topic or issue, I think there will be more response in discussions.

Questions 4 to 7 are based on the following conversation. At the end of the conversation, you will be given 20 seconds to answer the questions.

Now listen to the conversation.

Eileen: Jason, what do you think about friendship? Do you believe "a friend in need is a friend indeed?"

Jason: Well, Eileen, a true friend should be more than that.

Eileen: What do you mean?

Jason: A true friend should also be able to share your happy moments without feeling jealous, a true friend should also be able to forgive and tolerate, and a true friend should listen to you when you talk about your problems.

Eileen: You're a married man. How do you find your friendships?

Jason: Although my family life is fulfilling, it isn't enough. Both my wife and I get tremendous satisfaction from our friends, married and single, male or female. And we have our separate friends too.

Eileen: That's great.

Jason: Eileen, what's your view about friendship?

Eileen: I think a friend is one you can always count on. It's more important than love. If you love someone, you can always fall out of love again. But a real friend is a fiend for life.

Jason: That's well said.

Eileen: What do you think of online friendship?

Jason: The Internet makes it possible for me to make more friends than I otherwise would. But I have to cut down on my online time, or I would be overwhelmed with too many friends.

Eileen: Well, you don't have to, because the Internet is a virtual world and it's kind of difficult to put a friend to real test.

Questions 8 *to* 10 *are based on the following conversation. At the end of the conversation, you will be given* 15 *seconds to answer the questions.*

Now listen to the conversation.

Barbara: Welcome to visit our city, Mr. Lewis—but, of course, you have been here before, haven't you?

Lewis: Yes, I have, what a good memory you have! I was here for the Arts Festival last year.

Barbara: And what will you be doing this year?

Lewis: Oh, I came here primarily for a holiday and to see some friends. But I will also be giving private cello lessons as well.

126

Barbara: I believe that your cello is rather special. Is that true?

Lewis: Oh, yes. It was made for my uncle by a very expert German cello maker call Schuster. When I began cello lessons at the age of eight, he said that when I grew big enough to handle a full-sized cello, he would give it to me.

Barbara: So when a child begins to play the cello, he or she starts on a smaller instrument?

Lewis: Of course, or he would be very uncomfortable. Many children begin with half-sized cello, but as I was big for my age, I began with a two-thirds-sized cello.

Barbara: Are you going to other places on this trip and will you take your cello with you?

Lewis: Yes, very definitely.

Barbara: But, isn't it difficult taking a cello around with you?

Lewis: Not really. I just receive two seats when I'm traveling anywhere, one for me and one for my cello. It's such a precious instrument to me that it hardly ever leaves my side.

SECTION B PASSAGES

In this section, you will hear several passages. Listen to the passages carefully and then answer the questions that follow.

Questions 11 to 13 are based on the following passage. At the end of the passage, you will be given 15 seconds to answer the questions.

Now listen to the passage.

Eyes reveal our feelings and moods. We feel uneasy if we can not see the eyes of the person with whom we are talking. Similarly when the person avoids eye contact while speaking we tend to evaluate him/

127

her negatively. Avoiding eye contact is considered as a sign of dishonesty, lack of self-confidence and boredom.

Eye contact serves an important role in maintaining and initiating conversation. For example, when the speaker takes pause while talking and gazes at the listener it serves as a cue to the listener to speak.

People maintain more eye contact when they are interested in conversation or when they are seeking approval of others. It is difficult to ignore a person who looks directly at you while placing some request or demand.

Eye contact defines the nature and the intensity of interpersonal relations. Couples in love maintain more eye contact. It is also interesting to observe that the strangers gaze at each other when they are at distance but as they come closer they avoid eye contact. Eye contact also reflects status. People of high status maintain more eye contact while talking than while listening to the people of lower status.

Eyes are powerful communicators as they reflect our emotions. If someone smiles at us but his eyes do not reflect it we consider it a phony smile. When the expressions on our face are also reflected in our eyes they are taken as true feelings.

Questions 14 *to* 17 *are based on the following passage. At the end of the passage, you will be given* 20 *seconds to answer the questions.*

Now listen to the passage.

English is fast becoming the common language of the European Union, taking over from French as the preferred foreign language taught in schools and the workplace.

A third of EU citizens speak English as their best foreign language, compared to 9. 5 per cent for French, according to a poll of 16, 000 EU residents released by the European Commission yesterday. German is a distant fourth, preferred by only 4. 2 per cent.

The British are revealed as Europe's worst linguists. 65. 9 per cent the British admit that they cannot speak any other language. At the other extreme, 97. 8 per cent of Luxembourgeois speak other languages, typically French, German or English, as well as their native dialect Letzebuergesch.

Four fifths of Dutch, Danes and Swedes speak English, learning it intensively at school. The overwhelming majority agree that everybody in the EU should have a working knowledge of English. Even the French, the strongest defenders of linguistic tradition, accept by a margin of two to one that English is now a requirement.

The results suggest that English has already won the battle to become the administrative and business language, unifying Europe's professional classes.

Questions 18 *to* 20 *are based on the following passage. At the end of the passage, you will be given* 15 *seconds to answer the questions.*

Now listen to the passage.

Suicide is the number one killer of people aged 15~34 in China, particularly young women in rural areas. China's suicide rates are not exceptionally high compared with many other countries, but several factors make suicide a big public health problem.

First, the sheer size of China's population means the numbers are startling: More than 250,000 people commit suicide each year and two million more make the attempt. In addition, researchers say China is one of the few countries where more women kill themselves than men. Young, rural women are particularly at risk, and some observers say that may be because of their limited education, work and marriage options.

But Canadian psychiatrist Michael Phillips disagrees. He says that while more women than men attempt suicide in many other countries, in China they succeed more often. Because of the method they use, which is usually pesticides, and because of limited reviving abilities in rural areas, a lot more are dying.

While mental illness is a serious issue in China, Dr. Phillips cautions that it is not the cause of all suicides. Everybody in the West assumes that if somebody attempts or commits suicide, they have a mental illness—it's almost a required condition. In China, the attitude is very different—if you talk to people in rural and urban areas, it's always conflicts and failure at school and so on.

SECTION C   NEWS BROADCAST

Question 21 *is based on the following news. At the end of the news item, you will be given* 5 *seconds to answer the questions.*

Now listen to the news.

A new report released by the UNAIDS program and the World Health Organization says HIV infection rates and AIDS death continue to climb across the globe over the past twelve months. The global AIDS epidemic shows no signs of abating(减退). That's the conclusion of the latest report by the Joint UN Program on AIDS and World Health Organization. Timed for release a week ahead of the World AIDS Day, the report paints a grim picture of the growing impact of AIDS, especially in the developing world.

Questions 22 and 23 are based on the following news. At the end of the news item, you will be given 10 seconds to answer the questions.

Now listen to the news.

Australia has defeated India 4:2 at the Asian Men's Field Hockey Tournament being played in Kuala Lumpur, Malaysia. The Australians overcame a two-goal deficit Tuesday to win their second straight match. Earlier Lee Jung Seon scored two goals to help South Korea defeat Spain 4:1. After four matches Pakistan leads the ten-nation tournament with twelve points from four wins. Germany is second with nine points followed by Australia with seven.

Questions 24 and 25 are based on the following news. At the end of the news item, you will be given 10 seconds to answer the question.

Now listen to the news.

Two British men have been jailed for six years in India for sexually abusing boys at a homeless children's shelter in Mumbai, India. The two men were also fined $35,000 each. The court heard boys as young as eight who lived at the shelter set up by the two men. A committee would be formed to decide how the fines could be used to help the victims.

Questions 26 and 27 are based on the following news. At the end of the news item, you will be given 10 seconds to answer the questions.

Now listen to the news.

US space agency said a space probe crashed into the heart of a comet. The probe crashed into Comet Temple 1 at a speed of 37,000 kilometers an hour. One of the scientists said, "We hit it just exactly where we wanted to and the impact was bigger than I expected, and bigger than most of us expected. We've got all the data we could possibly ask for. " Scientists hope that by getting "under the skin" of Comet Temple 1, they can gain new information on how our Solar System was formed and perhaps even how life emerged in our corner of the Universe.

Questions 28 to 30 are based on the following news. At the end of the news item, you will be given 15 seconds to answer the questions.

Now listen to the news.

Physicians often recommend extra liquids for patients with respiratory infections such as colds. The idea is that they replace water lost from fever. But researchers point to evidence showing that during a respiratory infection, the body releases large amounts of a hormone that conserves water. They suggest that consuming additional water might lead to too much fluid in the body and loss of necessary salt.

The researchers note that they have not been able to find any studies showing whether higher fluid consumption during a respiratory illness is harmful or beneficial. However, they urge doctors to be cautious about such a recommendation until medical research can demonstrate for certain.

TAPESCRIPT OF PRACTICE TEST 5

PART Ⅰ DICTATION

Listen to the following passage. Altogether the passage will be read to you four times. During the first reading, which will be read at normal speed, listen and try to understand the meaning. For the second and third readings, the passage will be read sentence by sentence, or phrase by phrase, with intervals of 15 seconds. The last reading will be read at normal speed again and during this time you should check your work. You will then be given 2 minutes to check through your work once more.

Now listen to the passage.

HOW CIGARETTES BECAME POPULAR

Before 1915, cigarettes were not particularly popular. / However, beginning in World War I cigarettes sales rose sharply, / boosted by distribution to soldiers and sailors, / and an unprecedented cigarette advertising campaign. /

During the war, cigarettes were sent overseas to American troops free. / They were so much more convenient to smoke in the trenches than pipes or cigars. / Millions of soldiers thus took up cigarette smoking during the war/ and continued their habit once they returned home. /

The 20th century cigarette advertising campaign began right after World War I,/ capitalizing on the patriotism that accompanied the war effort. / The ads often featured testimonials by movie stars, athletes and even doctors,/ who went so far as to suggest that good health was the reward of smoking. / Some cigarette manufacturers made particularly bold health claims for their products, /advising that their brand could calm nerves/ or even prevent smoker's cough. /

The second and third readings. You should begin writing now.

The last reading. Now, you have two minutes to check through your work.

PART Ⅱ   LISTENING COMPREHENSION

In sections A, B and C you will hear everything once only. Listen carefully and then answer the questions that follow.

SECTION A   CONVERSATIONS

In this section you will hear several conversations. Listen to the conversations carefully and then answer the questions that follow.

Questions 1 to 3 are based on the following conversation. At the end of the conversation, you will be given 15 seconds to answer the questions.

Now listen to the conversation.

Peck: Hi, Lisa. Can you tell me about your college study?

Lisa: Well, my college study may be a little bit different from what you think.

Peck: How?

Lisa: I don't have a fixed schedule like many students do. We don't have formal exams, which suits me, as I was never any good at exams. It's the course work that is important.

Peck: Currently you're on work placement, right?

Lisa: Yeah. My work placement is twice a week at a travel agency. Although I don't get paid it gives me a good experience of the job.

Peck: So you can travel to some places?

Lisa: You bet. We do go on educational trips, but there is plenty of time to hit the beach and do shopping. And the best thing was the tutors are laid back and are having a good time with us.

Peck: Seems you enjoy your school very much?

Lisa: Is there any better way to attend college than the freedom you enjoy where you can pretty much decide everything for yourself?

Questions 4 *to* 7 *are based on the following conversation. At the end of the conversation, you will be given* 20 *seconds to answer the questions.*

Now listen to the conversation.

Molly: Peter, people around the world come to America to live, work and study, so to understand America in terms of its cultural differences is very important.

Peter: I couldn't agree with you more, Molly. Americans are much more assertive than most foreigners. For example, Americans begin a discussion with a focus on accomplishments and concrete facts.

Molly: You're right. America is a rather individualistic society, with less social pressure to conform. So you will need to become more assertive and to speak out on your own behalf.

Peter: Another aspect of American behavior is Americans are more guarded about personal space. So when you are talking to an American, don't stay too close. This personal distance is not due to body odor or bad breath, but because closeness lends a sense of intimacy that is out of proportion to the relationship at the moment.

Molly: Yes. Also, try to avoid physical contact while you are speaking. Touching is a bit too intimate for casual acquaintances. So don't put your arm around their shoulder, touch their face, or hold their hand. Shaking hands when you initially meet or part is acceptable, but this is only momentary.

Peter: In many cultures, eye contact is a sign of disrespect, which is not the case in America. In fact, it is an indication of openness, honesty, and enthusiasm.

Questions 8 to 10 are based on the following conversation. At the end of the conversation, you will be given 15 seconds to answer the questions.

Now listen to the conversation.

Cathy: Hi, Warren.

Warren: Hi, Cathy.

Cathy: What do you think of the movie we saw last night? Do you like it?

Warren: Not really. It seemed like the director was trying so hard to impress us with unconventional dialogue that we didn't know what the story was. I think it was really boring.

Cathy: I think the movie was really thought provoking. I love it when a movie makes you think. It's a nice change from the superficial dialogue and boring characters you usually see in films these days.

Warren: I don't really care for non-traditional films. They are so depressing. The characters are always so intense.

Cathy: You got a point, but mainstream cinema is nothing but gun fights and car chasing. I get so sick of movies like that. I prefer movies with substance.

Warren: But sometimes you don't want to think; sometimes you just want a light movie. Like that comedy movie with Jim Carrey. I laughed throughout the movie.

Cathy: Movies have to be more than entertaining to me.

Warren: Did you see that new mystery movie that came out last month? That was so suspenseful. I was on the edge of my seat the whole time.

Cathy: I loved that movie. The plot was great, and the acting was incredible. I wouldn't be surprised if it were nominated for an Academy Award.

SECTION B   PASSAGES

In this section, you will hear several passages. Listen to the passages carefully and then answer the questions that follow.

Questions 11 to 13 are based on the following passage. At the end of the passage, you will be given 15 seconds to answer the questions.

Now listen to the passage.

Food supply is very important in explaining the behavior of many animals. In many parts of Africa, for example, large numbers of different animals move from place to place looking for the best grass and plants to eat. Every year large numbers of elephants and other animals move, at the same time, from one place to another where food supply is better. The land they move away from is given a chance to rest so that the grass and plants can grow fully again and will offer a good supply of food at the same time next year.

In some parts of Africa, where these migrations have been taking place naturally for so long, there is now a new problem. Men have started cattle farming and these cattle are killing the grass and plants. The wild animals have mouths which are shaped so that they do not pull up all of these grass and plants. So the grass and plants are not killed and can grow again. But the cattle have mouths which pull up all of the grass and plants and so kill them. If this goes on for long all the grass will die and there will be no food for either the wild animals or the cattle.

Questions 14 *to* 17 *are based on the following passage. At the end of the passage, you will be given* 20 *seconds to answer the questions.*

Now listen to the passage.

In Britain, just after the main television news programs, audience figures rise. It's weather forecast time. The BBC broadcasts forty-four live forecasts a day, 433 hours of weather a year, using forecasts from the Meteorological Office. The Met. Office makes predictions about he weather seven days in advance. These are based on observations from the ground, from satellites and from radar. The observations are stored in computers that can do up to 4,000 million calculations a second.

In Britain the weather is news. A television weather forecast often begins with an interesting fact—the town with the top temperature of the day or the place with the most rain. "The public like that kind of information," says senor forecaster Bill Giles. The BBC forecasters are professional meteorologists, but they do not have an easy job. They are the only presenters on television who do not use a script, and they cannot see a map that they are describing. Viewers are often critical, especially of female presenters. One woman left her job after rude letters and press reports about her clothes.

The British talk about the weather more than almost any other subject, so it is a surprise to discover that seventy percent of television viewers cannot remember what they saw on the weather forecast. "What happens is that people like watching and hearing forecasts, but they probably only take real notice when they need to," says one forecaster. "Or, of course, when we make mistakes!"

Questions 18 *to* 20 *are based on the following passage. At the end of the passage, you will be given* 15 *seconds to answer the questions.*

Now listen to the passage.

A new global health study shows that heart disease is an overlooked problem in developing countries. Low and middle-income nations suffer the overwhelming majority of deaths from heart diseases, including stroke. It shows that developing countries account for 80 percent of the world's 17 million heart disease and stroke deaths each year.

The rise in heart disease is linked to increasing urbanization and wealth around the world. Big cities are very economically efficient, but they do create an environment where people tend to eat more than they need, where food is cheap, where cigarette smoking becomes more frequent, and where because everything is close, they do not exercise as much, or use a car instead of feet or a bicycle.

In South Africa, for example, heart disease kills 75 percent more men aged 34 to 65 each year than in the United States. In India, the death rate is 44 percent higher; and in Brazil, 27 percent higher. Only China has a lower heart disease rate than the United States.

The victims in developing nations are of prime working age, thus taking a heavy toll on labor productivity. In contrast, wealthy industrial countries, through prevention and treatment, have reduced heart disease so most patients are elderly people.

SECTION C   NEWS BROADCAST

Questions 21 to 23 are based on the following news. At the end of the news item, you will be given 15 seconds to answer the questions.

Now listen to the news.

A woman in England has been seriously attacked after accepting a lift from a man. The victim got into the car and before long she was attacked by the man. She fought him off and the manreceived deep bites into the fingers of his right hand. The woman got out of the car and asked for help. The attacker is believed to be aged in his 20s to 30s, has dirty fair hair, with bulging eyes and a large red nose. He is also believed to have spoken with a southern Irish accent. The incident took place at about 23:45 GMT on Saturday and police have asked for information about the silver car the man was driving.

Questions 24 and 25 are based on the following news. At the end of the news item, you will be given 10 seconds to answer the questions.

Now listen to the news.

Two men were killed in a road accident in County Londonderry while being chased by police. Police were chasing their vehicle when it hit a bus on the Hillhead Road. Five vehicles were caught up in the accident. Two people in the bus were taken to hospital, while three others were treated at the scene for shock. There were unconfirmed

140

reports that the dead men had been travelling in a car stolen on Thursday. Police were following the car because it had been speeding.

Questions 26 and 27 are based on the following news. At the end of the news item, you will be given 10 seconds to answer the question.

Now listen to the news.

A 30-year-old woman from Egypt died of bird flu this week. Reports said the woman, who kept a chicken farm despite a ban on the practice, died of a fever at Cairo's main hospital on Friday. Egypt last month ordered the killing of all chicken kept in homes, as part of efforts to stop the spread of the H5N1 strain of the bird flu virus. The H5N1 strain has killed at least 90 people since early 2003, mostly in South-East Asia. The virus can infect humans in close contact with birds. There is still no evidence that it can be passed from human to human.

Questions 28 and 29 are based on the following news. At the end of the news item, you will be given 10 seconds to answer the questions.

Now listen to the news.

There are fears that the implementation of the Kyoto Treaty on tackling global warming may have been dealt a fatal blow after President Putin's economic advisor said Russia would not ratify(批准)it because it would severely hold back Russia's economic growth. The Kyoto Treaty sets limits on carbon dioxide emissions. To come into effect it must be ratified by enough countries that cover 55 percent of emissions. Since the United States rejected the treaty, this can only happen with Russia's participation.

Question 30 *is based on the following news. At the end of the news item, you will be given* 5 *seconds to answer the questions.*
Now listen to the news.

The World Trade Organization has finally approved a deal in Geneva which gives poorer nations access to cheap drugs to fight diseases such as AIDS and tuberculosis(肺结核). In a deal hailed by the WTO as historic, countries unable to manufacture medicines domestically will be allowed to ignore international patents and import cheap copies of drugs. The deal was worked out between key developing countries and the United States after Washington agreed to relax rules protecting drug patents.

TAPESCRIPT OF PRACTICE TEST 6

PART I DICTATION

Listen to the following passage. Altogether the passage will be read to you four times. During the first reading, which will be read at normal speed, listen and try to understand the meaning. For the second and third readings, the passage will be read sentence by sentence, or phrase by phrase, with intervals of 15 seconds. The last reading will be read at normal speed again and during this time you should check your work. You will then be given 2 minutes to check through your work once more.

Now listen to the passage.

WOMEN AND FASHION

If women are exploited year after year,/ they have only themselves to blame. / Because they tremble at being seen in public in clothes that are out of fashion,/ they are always taken advantage of by the designers and the big stores. / Clothes which have been worn only a few times/ have to be put aside because of the change of fashion. /

Changing fashions are nothing more than the intentional creation of waste. / Many women spend vast sums of money each year/ to replace clothes that have hardly been worn. / Women who cannot afford to throw away clothing in this way,/ waste hours of their time altering the dresses they have. / Fashion designers are rarely concerned with vital things like warmth and comfort. / They are only interested in outward appearance/ and they exploit women who will put up with any amount of discomfort,/ as long as they look right. /

The second and third readings. You should begin writing now.

The last reading. Now, you have two minutes to check through your work.

PART II LISTENING COMPREHENSION

In sections A, B and C you will hear everything once only. Listen carefully and then answer the questions that follow.

SECTION A CONVERSATIONS

In this section you will hear several conversations. Listen to the conversations carefully and then answer the questions that follow.

Questions 1 to 3 are based on the following conversation. At the end of the conversation, you will be given 15 seconds to answer the questions.

Now listen to the conversation.

Terry: Emily, I guess you don't drink.

Emily: Not really. I don't drink every night, but if I've had a particularly bad day, I definitely will have one or two glasses of wine. And I tend to drink a little bit more at weekends. How about you?

Terry: I try not to drink too much during the week, but I like to have five to six glasses of wine at weekends.

Emily: But why do we drink in the first place?

Terry: I think people drink first of all to quench(止渴)thirst. Also drinking can make us feel good because some chemicals are activated in our brain.

Emily: But how much should we drink?

Terry: A glass of wine isn't going to damage our body. It's fine.

144

But many people don't know their daily allowance(定量).

Emily: Talking about allowance, glass is not a standard measurement, because the same glass can have different strength of alcohol.

Terry: That's right. People generally use "unit" to describe the strength of a wine or beer. So the recommended daily alcohol allowance is three to four units for men and two to three for women.

Emily: Drinking more than that must be harmful to our body.

Terry: Yes. The liver can only process one unit of alcohol per hour. So if you have twenty units of alcohol inside you it'll take twenty-four hours for the alcohol to be processed by the liver. Anyone who drinks is increasing the risk of damaging their body if they go above twenty-one to twenty-eight units of alcohol a week.

Questions 4 to 7 are based on the following conversation. At the end of the conversation, you will be given 20 seconds to answer the questions.

Now listen to the conversation.

Margaret: Hi, Terry, you're just back from New York?

Terry: Yes, Margaret.

Margaret: It must be an exciting trip.

Terry: Well, I've really seen lots of things. I saw the most spectacular view when I was crossing a bridge to Manhattan at dusk, and the skyscrapers were lit up producing a classic nighttime view of Manhattan.

Margaret: That's really beautiful.

Terry: But that's not the whole picture. Some of the streets in

New York are very rough. I saw large piles of garbage bags at the roadside, and graffiti all over garage doors and store shutters.

Margaret: I can't believe it.

Terry: The garbage are tidily bagged and boxed, though.

Margaret: Did you stay in a hotel?

Terry: Yes. The hotel we stayed at turned out to be fairly decent, though the room was small, with a tiny bathroom that was only about 3 feet larger than the bed. As I was inexperienced with tourist-area hotels, I was startled, I mean, the room was $129 a night. But at least the room was clean and the bed reasonably comfortable.

Margaret: What's your general impression of New York?

Terry: Well, restaurants pack their tiny tables very tightly; grocery stores and bookstores have aisles that are narrow; the sidewalks are cluttered with newsstands, vendors and their carts, and places that aren't restrictively small, such as the lawns around the Natural History Museum, are full of people, so they's no escape.

Questions 8 to 10 are based on the following conversation. At the end of the conversation, you will be given 15 seconds to answer the questions.

Now listen to the conversation.

Sally: Terry, you had an encounter with an elephant yesterday?

Terry: yeah, it scared me to death.

Sally: What happened?

Terry: I was walking in the park when a female elephant came charging at me from behind.

Sally: How terrifying!

Terry: Yes. As I was running I tripped and fell to the ground. Just as I turned around the tusks were already about a foot from my chest.

Sally: She was trying to stab you with her tusks?

Terry: She was going for a kill. I just had time to grab the tusks and kind of pulled them past my body. And one tusk stabbed into the earth about a few centimeters from my head. I held on and she just tried to stab me. Miraculously she didn't touch anything vital.

Sally: When she stabbed into the earth, she must have been right on top of you?

Terry: Oh yes, she was. Her eyeballs were about two inches from my eyeballs.

Sally: Just at that second when you were staring at her in the eye, was there anything going through your head or were you overwhelmed with terror?

Terry: My thought was, if you let go these tusks, you are dead meat.

Sally: Well, what did happen? Why didn't you die?

Terry: Usually the elephant is just as scared as you are. Someone came up and screamed at the elephant. That probably distracted her and she decided to run away.

SECTION B PASSAGES

In this section, you will hear several passages. Listen to the passages carefully and then answer the questions that follow.

Questions 11 to 13 are based on the following passage. At the end of the passage, you will be given 15 seconds to answer the questions.

Now listen to the passage.

You probably know that the chameleon can change its color to blend with its surroundings. But did you know that it has a tongue that is longer than its whole body? It is probably the fastest tongue on earth. The chameleon can shoot it out at an incredible speed to capture an insect.

In every other respect the chameleon is a very slow creature. It spends most of its time sitting motionless on branches of bushes or trees, and when it does change its position, it moves extremely slowly. But it has two mobile and efficient eyes. These move independently of each other, so that the chameleon can see in every direction without moving its head at all. A motionless body is of course very valuable, as it does not frighten away the insects that are its prey.

When an insect settles within range, the chameleon opens its mouth slightly and you can see the pink tongue. The naked eye cannot see what happens next. It happens so rapidly that only a high-speed camera can record the action. All that the human watcher can see is the tongue going back into the chameleon's mouth and its jaw snapping shut. The insect, however, has disappeared and the chameleon is now chewing it.

Questions 14 to 17 are based on the following passage. At the end of the passage, you will be given 20 seconds to answer the questions.

Now listen to the passage.

There is probably no area of human activity in which our values and lifestyles are reflected more vividly than they are in the clothes

148

that we choose to wear. The dress of an individual is a kind of "sign language" that communicates a complex set of information and is usually the basis on which immediate impressions are formed. Traditionally a concern for clothes was considered to be a feminine preoccupation, while men took pride in the fact that they were completely lacking in clothes consciousness.

Time has changed as masculine dress takes on greater variety and color. As early as 1955, a research revealed that men attached high importance to the value of clothing in daily life. White-collar workers in particular viewed dress as a symbol capable of manipulation, that could be used to impress or influence others, especially in the work situation. Although blue-collar workers were less aware that they might be judged on the basis of their clothing, they recognized that any difference from the accepted pattern of dress would draw ridicule from fellow workers.

Since that time, the pattern have changed: the typical office worker may now be wearing the blue shirt, and the laborer a white shirt; but the importance of dress has not diminished.

Questions 18 to 20 are based on the following passage. At the end of the passage, you will be given 15 seconds to answer the questions.

Now listen to the passage.

New York State has passed the United States' first state law banning motorists talking on hand-held cell phones. The ban will begin November 1, although drivers caught using hand-held cell phones will be given only warnings during the first month

First-time violators will face a $100 fine. A second violation calls for a $200 fine and every following violation will cost $500.

149

At least a dozen local areas have established bans, starting in 1999; and 40 states have had bans proposed but not passed. At least 23 countries, including the Great Britain, Italy, Israel and Japan, ban drivers from using hand-held cell phones.

There are about 115 million cell phones in use in the United States and more than 6 million in New York State.

"To think that I'm not going to use cell phone when at the same time I can still use my laptop, I still can read a paper, I can still change my pants while driving 65 mph. I think there's just something wrong," an official said.

Other critics noted that other things like eating, drinking coffee and applying make-up while driving posed at least as much of a concern. They suggested that the ban include a broader range of things.

SECTION C　NEWS BROADCAST

Question 21 *is based on the following news. At the end of the news item, you will be given* 5 *seconds to answer the questions.*

Now listen to the news.

Scientists from South Korea say they have managed to clone and grow human embryos(胚胎)for the first time to create cells which could eventually be used to treat a whole range of diseases. The researchers have shown they could produce stem cells(干细胞)from human embryos which can then be grown into any cell in the body and not be rejected if transplanted back. The scientists say the aim of the procedure is not to create a human being but for medical uses in what is called therapeutic(治疗的)cloning.

Questions 22 *and* 23 *are based on the following news. At the end*

*of the news item, you will be given 10 seconds to answer the
questions.*

Now listen to the news.

American officials are investigating the first ever suspected case
of mad cow disease. The potential case was discovered in a single
cow.

The American Agriculture Secretary Ann Veneman has said that
preliminary tests indicate that a single cow from a farm in Washington
state may have mad cow disease. She says the test was taken on the
ninth of December and now further testing is required for definite
confirmation. Ms. Veneman reassures the public that it cannot yet be
confirmed this was an isolated case, but since 1990 steps have been
taken to ensure there could be no spread of the disease through
American herds as had taken place in Britain.

*Questions 24 to 26 are based on the following news. At the end
of the news item, you will be given 15 seconds to answer the
question.*

Now listen to the news.

The United States' five-year productivity growth came to a stop
at the end of 2005. For the final three months of 2005, productivity
fell 0.6%, the first such slide since early 2001. Economists said the
decline could be the result of factors such as the effect of Hurricane
Katrina. The slowdown in productivity means the cost of labour will
rise, which could cause inflation. Salary growth in the US remains
low, with 2005 producing the smallest rise in wages since 1996.

Questions 27 to 28 are based on the following news. At the end of the news item, you will be given 10 seconds to answer the questions.

Now listen to the news.

The American space agency NASA says its Mars probe(探测器) Opportunity has found evidence that there was once enough liquid water on the planet for life to have existed. But at a news conference in Washington NASA scientists said the probe had found no direct evidence of life itself.

NASA scientists say they have hard evidence that Mars was once extremely wet and certainly able to support life. The claim is based on data gathered by their robotic probe Opportunity which landed by chance in a rocky area. Instruments on board have been studying the chemical makeup of the rock and examining it with a microscope. Researchers say the findings show that there could once be a lake here or hot springs. A European satellite in orbit around Mars detected water in the atmosphere and ice in the soil in January, but this is the first time that scientists have claimed that they found a specific site on the planet that could definitely have harbored life.

Questions 29 and 30 are based on the following news. At the end of the news item, you will be given 10 seconds to answer the questions.

Now listen to the news.

France has carried out the first of a planned series of nuclear tests in the south Pacific despite strong international opposition. The French Defence Minister said the device exploded at an underground site beneath Mururoa Atoll yielded less than 20 kilotons. Australian scientists described it as fairly small compared with previous tests.

There's been swift reaction from several countries. New Zealand and Chile have recalled their ambassadors to Paris in protest. Australia condemned the test and the US expressed its regret. Before the nuclear device was exploded, the French President Jacques Chirac said his country might carry out fewer than eight tests originally planned.

TAPESCRIPT OF PRACTICE TEST 7

PART I DICTATION

Listen to the following passage. Altogether the passage will be read to you four times. During the first reading, which will be read at normal speed, listen and try to understand the meaning. For the second and third readings, the passage will be read sentence by sentence, or phrase by phrase, with intervals of 15 seconds. The last reading will be read at normal speed again and during this time you should check your work. You will then be given 2 minutes to check through your work once more.

Now listen to the passage.

MUSHROOMS

Every year mushrooms of every size and shape/ push their way up from under dead leaves or from inside dead trees. /

The yearly growing season begins in late summer and continues through autumn. / During that brief period, people who like to eat mushrooms/ spend a lot of time walking through fields and forests. / They look for what some people call "the food of the gods. "/

Mushrooms grow on dead organic matter. / They are formed by spores. /These spores are produced by fully grown mushrooms. / They fall from the underside of the top of a mushroom. / The wind spreads them over a wide area. / When they land on a tree that has fallen, they begin to grow. /

The hunt for wild mushrooms has taken place throughout the world since ancient times. / And, like most hunts, there is some danger. / People have to be careful not to eat mushrooms that are

154

poisonous. /

The second and third readings. You should begin writing now.

The last reading. Now, you have two minutes to check through *your work.*

PART Ⅱ LISTENING COMPREHENSION

In sections A, B and C you will hear everything once only. *Listen carefully and then answer the questions that follow.*

SECTION A CONVERSATIONS

In this section you will hear several conversations. Listen to the *conversations carefully and then answer the questions that follow.*

Questions 1 to 3 are based on the following conversation. At the *end of the conversation, you will be given 15 seconds to answer the* *questions.*

Now listen to the conversation.

Host: Dr. Johnson, Can we talk a little bit about bad manners in Asia?

Dr. Johnson: Sure.

Host: What's really bad manners in South Korea?

Dr. Johnson: Well, I think it really depends on your upbringing. Some people might find eating habits, you know, some people like to slurp their food, which makes lots of noise, others like to, say, for instance, wear white socks with their suits, which is considered a big social mistake by some people.

Host: What's bad manners in Japan?

Dr. Johnson: One thing that's acceptable in the west but not acceptable in Japan is blowing your nose. If you blow your

155

nose on a date, then you can...

Host: You blow the date.

Dr. Johnson: Yes.

Host: People in Malaysia care very much about their table manners?

Dr. Johnson: Yes. Eating your food too loudly and not caring for your guests are considered bad manners. If you don't serve your guests before you start eating food, that's pretty bad table manners. But also other problems of bad habits include whether you take into account the personal spaces that people have and whether you get too close.

Host: Can people in Japan kiss in public, in a park, for example?

Dr. Johnson: Actually Japanese parks are designed and used for that purpose. People go to the parks to make out. This is why they have an entire magazine dedicated to this public display of affection. But making out is not allowed anywhere else in Japan. It's very strange.

Questions 4 to 7 are based on the following conversation. At the end of the conversation, you will be given 20 seconds to answer the questions.

Now listen to the conversation.

Kerry: Laura, you're fat for your age.

Laura: I know, and I'm thinking about it all the time.

Kerry: But it isn't that serious.

Laura: Well, I've always been self-conscious about my weight and appearance. Though I've never thought of myself as ugly, I've always thought of myself as slightly overweight.

Kerry: Why are you so self-conscious?

Laura: I grew up watching my mother struggle with her weight and her poor opinion of her appearance. I remember watching her try the occasional diet and never getting anywhere. My grandmother, who lived with us, also would go on diet and loose large amounts of weight, only to put it back on.

Kerry: Are you always fat?

Laura: No. When I moved away to a larger city with my boyfriend, we indulged regularly in fast food and alcohol simply because we could. We'd order 2 large pizzas at a time. I'd go to the local bakery to pick up 2 boxes of mini doughnuts because they had buy-one-get-one-free specials. One box would be gone before my boyfriend even got home.

Kerry: You got to change that.

Laura: That is the hardest part. We've got the genes that make us forever want to eat more, something that allowed our ancestors to survive in times of starvation. So it's something that can even bend your strongest will.

Questions 8 to 10 are based on the following conversation. At the end of the conversation, you will be given 15 seconds to answer the questions.

Now listen to the conversation.

Cathy: John, can you tell me about the differences many foreign students encounter in American classrooms?

John: One of the first things that happen is that the teacher tells the students to call him or her by their first name. The teacher will then ask the students what they want to be called. Most of them will follow the teacher's example and they'll have the teacher call them by their first names, even if this isn't customary in the country where they come form.

Cathy: Do they have a problem with that?

John: For some students it sticks in their throat (说不出口) to have to call their teacher by his or her first name and some never quite get comfortable with that.

Cathy: Are teachers very formal in class?

John: Teachers are very forthcoming (直率), you know, talking about themselves, their children, their dogs. It's a wonderful way of motivating students and getting them to feel good in the classroom.

Cathy: The classroom must look informal, too?

John: Yes. The chairs are not organized in rows. They might be organized in a circle or in a semi-circle. There might be large tables in a classroom where students sit in groups around the table. And there is a reason for this kind of classroom organization. It comes back to the idea that learning is a participatory activity, it is something that goes both ways.

Cathy: With this kind of informality, I guess American teachers don't mind students not being punctual for class.

John: American teachers are fastidious (要求极高的) about punctuality. If students don't show up on time, it conveys an attitude of disrespect to the professor.

SECTION B   PASSAGES

In this section, you will hear several passages. Listen to the passages carefully and then answer the questions that follow.

Questions 11 *to* 13 *are based on the following passage. At the end of the passage, you will be given* 15 *seconds to answer the questions.*

Now listen to the passage.

158

A dog may be man's best friend, but new archaeological evidence from Cyprus shows that the human relationship with cats is also very old, in fact, much older than thought. The discovery of a cat skeleton by French scientists pushes the known date of cats as pets back more than 5,000 years.

The sound of the home cat has been familiar to people for ages. The ancient Egyptians are generally thought to have been the first to tame and breed them to produce a new species about 4,000 years ago. But researchers have long suspected that wild cats began associating with humans much earlier, although they had limited evidence.

Now, scientists from the French National Museum of Natural History in Paris have discovered such clues. They uncovered the remains of a cat buried on the Mediterranean island of Cyprus. A cat skeleton was found alongside that of a human and a rich variety of offerings, and it showed no signs of butchering. This suggests that people had developed a special relationship with cats by that distant time.

The discovery of the cat skeleton with the human skeleton is much stronger evidence of taming. The cat does not look different from a wild cat, but the context of the discovery shows the tight relationship between a human and the cat.

Questions 14 to 17 are based on the following passage. At the end of the passage, you will be given 20 seconds to answer the questions.

Now listen to the passage.

Not every service or product meets your satisfaction. When you are dissatisfied, you should voice your dissatisfaction. One reason for doing so is to help the vendor know there is a problem. The problem may have been created at a lower level in the vendor's company, and the vendor himself may know nothing about it at all. You help him when you bring weaknesses of failures to his attention.

A second reason for writing a letter of complaint to a vendor is to seek compensation. You may not wish to pursue the matter so far as to take legal action, but you may wish to give the vendor the opportunity of making good. Most vendors value your business and their reputation sufficiently to replace defective goods or refund money when necessary. No vendor likes to do so, but your carefully worded letter of complaint may motivate him to do so.

When you write a letter of complaint, you'd better keep these tips in mind: First, be polite though firm. You will not win a vendor's cooperation by anger. Secondly, be reasonable. Show logically and factually that the fault lies with the vendor. The vendor should be impressed with your fairness and good grasp of the facts in the matter. Thirdly, be specific about what is wrong and what you want done about it. Lastly, tell how you have been hurt or inconvenienced by the problem. This strengthens your argument for compensation.

Questions 18 to 20 are based on the following passage. At the end of the passage, you will be given 15 seconds to answer the questions.

Now listen to the passage.

Is vitamin E a cure for baldness? Can vitamin E relieve the pain of arthritis? These are only a few of the uses some people claim for vitamin E, but for many years no scientific proof has been possible for any of these claim.

In humans, with one exception, there are no symptoms of any

160

kind associated with a vitamin E deficiency. Premature infants who lack proper amounts of vitamin E sometimes develop anemia or skin rashes, but many symptoms caused by this deficiency in human adults are either too insignificant to appear in normal tests or are simply nonexistent.

Some studies have found vitamin E helpful in treating specific diseases, such as angina pectoris(心肌梗塞), a type of heart disease. But other studies have tried to duplicate these findings and failed. So there is no absolutely undeniable evidence that vitamin E will prevent or cure disease.

Claims for the cosmetic use of vitamin E continue to multiply, however. Creams containing vitamin E appear on the market almost daily, to help remove skin blemishes, to help soften dry skin, to control skin wrinkles. Vitamin E is even used in deodorants(除味剂). Vitamin E itself is an antioxidant, so the producers believe that vitamin E will prevent odor by preventing bacteria from oxidizing sweat. But no study or medical proof ever appeared to prove any of these cosmetic claims completely.

You can add vitamin E pills to your morning routine if you like, but unfortunately no one has ever been able to demonstrate conclusively any reason why you should.

SECTION C　NEWS BROADCAST

Questions 21 and 22 are based on the following news. At the end of the news item, you will be given 10 seconds to answer the questions.

Now listen to the news.

A powerful tropical cyclone has hit Australia's north-east coast, causing winds of up to 290 kilometers an hour. Tropical Cyclone

Larry smashed into Queensland, making thousands homeless. About a dozen people suffered minor injuries and up to 50,000 homes are without power. A state of emergency has been declared and Prime Minister John Howard has promised help for the affected areas. The damage to houses is very extensive, but there have not been any very serious injuries.

Questions 23 and 24 are based on the following news. At the end of the news item, you will be given 10 seconds to answer the questions.

Now listen to the news.

Women aged 18 to 24 are drinking more than men of the same age in the UK. This is the result of a major international study focusing on 12 European countries in 2004 and 2005.

Analysis of a Europe-wide study also shows that alcohol consumption in southern Mediterranean countries is falling, but rising in northern Europe. In the past in Britain, women tended to drink in a much safer way than men, possibly because they feared for their physical safety when they did. But this does not seem to be as much of an issue for them now.

Questions 25 and 26 are based on the following news. At the end of the news item, you will be given 10 seconds to answer the question.

Now listen to the news.

An influential aid organization in Australia reports that the health of many of the country's indigenous(土著的)people is worse than that of people in the developing world. The Fred Hollows

Foundation is demanding an emergency summit to address the problem. The foundation says statistics show that aboriginal(土著的) health is worse than the health of people in such poor countries as Bangladesh, Nepal and Sudan.

The reasons are thought to be social rather than a lack of health care in remote communities. Poor housing, hygiene, a lack of employment and education along with a reliance on convenience food combine to cause long-term health problems for young aborigines.

Question 27 is based on the following news. At the end of the news item, you will be given 5 seconds to answer the questions.
Now listen to the news.

US car manufacturer General Motors has said it expects to make 4 billion dollars this year from a significant cost-cutting plan. The carmaker made a 3. 8 billion dollars loss in the first quarter because of falling US sales. The US car giant has suffered in the face of fierce competition from Asian rivals and changing consumer tastes.

Questions 28 to 30 are based on the following news. At the end of the news item, you will be given 15 seconds to answer the questions.
Now listen to the news.

A new government study shows that most U. S. corporations paid no federal taxes between 1996 and 2000. The study found that more than 60 percent of U. S.-based companies avoided federal taxes altogether. The percentage of foreign-owned firms that paid zero taxes was about 10 percent higher. The study also showed that many firms that did pay taxes, paid less than the standard 35 percent federal income tax on corporations. A front-page article in Tuesday's Wall Street Journal says the study shows that evading taxes, through legal or other means, has become "deeply rooted in U. S. corporate culture".

TAPESCRIPT OF PRACTICE TEST 8

PART I DICTATION

Listen to the following passage. Altogether the passage will be read to you four times. During the first reading, which will be read at normal speed, listen and try to understand the meaning. For the second and third readings, the passage will be read sentence by sentence, or phrase by phrase, with intervals of 15 seconds. The last reading will be read at normal speed again and during this time you should check your work. You will then be given 2 minutes to check through your work once more.

Now listen to the passage.

WORDS

How men first learnt to invent words is unknown. / What we do known is that men somehow invented certain sounds/ to express thoughts and feelings, actions, and things,/ so that they could communicate with each other. / Later people agreed upon certain signs, called letters,/ which could be combined to represent those sounds,/ and which could be written down. / These sounds, whether spoken or written in letters, we call words. / The power of words, then, lies in their associations/—the things they bring up before our minds. / Words become filled with meaning for us by experience. / Great writers are those who not only have great thoughts/ but also express these thoughts in words which appeal powerfully to our minds and emotions. / This charming and telling use of words is called literary style. / We should therefore learn to choose our words carefully and use them accurately,/ or they will make our speech silly and vulgar. /

The second and third readings. You should begin writing now.

The last reading. Now, you have two minutes to check through your work.

PART Ⅱ LISTENING COMPREHENSION

In sections A, B and C you will hear everything once only. Listen carefully and then answer the questions that follow.

SECTION A CONVERSATIONS

In this section you will hear several conversations. Listen to the conversations carefully and then answer the questions that follow.

Questions 1 to 3 are based on the following conversation. At the end of the conversation, you will be given 15 seconds to answer the questions.

Now listen to the conversation.

Bill: Greta, it's very sad that literature seems to have gone out of favor these days.

Greta: That's right. Literature has become a dispensable activity. No doubt it is useful for cultivating sensitivity and good manners, but essentially it is something that resembles sports, the movies, or a game of chess.

Bill: What has happened?

Greta: People nowadays are so preoccupied with their struggle of life that they cannot waste their precious time buried in a novel, a book of poetry, or a literary essay for hours and hours.

Bill: Surely literature has its values.

Greta: That's right. Literature provides common ground where

166

human beings may recognize themselves, no matter how different their professions, their geographical locations, their personal circumstances.

Bill: Yes. As readers of Shakespeare and Tolstoy, we understand each other across space and time, and we feel ourselves to be members of the same species.

Greta: Another benefit of literature is at the level of language. A person who reads literary texts can cultivate his language of communication, making it richer and more precise.

Bill: To be able to find the appropriate expression for every idea and every emotion.

Greta: Still another benefit of literature is that literature cultivates the critical mind. This is because all good literature is radical, and poses radical questions about the world in which we live.

Bill: Yes. Literature is not intended for those human beings who are satisfied with their lot(命运), who are content with life as they now live it.

Questions 4 to 7 are based on the following conversation. At the end of the conversation, you will be given 20 seconds to answer the questions.

Now listen to the conversation.

Larry: Susan, I'm going to college next month. What are the things I should bring with me or leave behind?

Susan: You should bring a new personality. I'm not saying that you should be something that you are not. However, college is an opportunity to change yourself. From day one, don't think of college as 13th grade but the first step in the new you.

Larry: That's a good idea. What else?

Susan: Bring a working camera.

Larry: Why?

Susan: Well, you pay $30,000 per year on tuition and expenses. What's another $100 in photos. Plus, you can mail photos to your family and relatives and get money from them. In that sense, this $100 investment can return thousands of dollars.

Larry: That's a wonderful idea.

Susan: Also bring a microwave and a mini-fridge. Your cafeteria may cater to your taste, but there will be days when you don't feel like getting out of your room. Also, you might get some late night food cravings.

Larry: What should I not bring to college?

Susan: Your high school date if you have one.

Larry: Why?

Susan: Having a high school relationship limits your ability to meet other people. Unless you feel that you are destined with your high school sweetheart, it is probably better for both of you to venture out into the college social scene.

Questions 8 to 10 are based on the following conversation. At the end of the conversation, you will be given 15 seconds to answer the questions.

Now listen to the conversation.

Karen: Alan, do you like celebrities?

Alan: I'm fascinated with them. I often read the stories about their lives and their hobbies.

Karen: Why should we care about celebrities? When they were born, they were no different than any of us. Just because they have a camera on them doesn't mean that they have to be ideal citizens.

Alan: I think many celebrities have fascinating stories, and to read these stories can be very inspirational. They forever inspire us to achieve more.

Karen: So you hold celebrities as your role models?

Alan: Yes. But celebrities definitely should consider how their behavior will be seen by those who have chosen them as a role model.

Karen: But don't you think celebrities also make us spend money? I mean we have to follow their lavish lifestyles.

Alan: Although I may be fascinated with celebrities' lifestyles, I stop short of imitating them.

Karen: I think it's all right to have a normal interest in actors and artists we're fond of, but if you know more about Britney Spears than your next-door neighbor, you need help.

Alan: I think too that the most important people in our lives should be our friends and family. But celebrities do keep us entertained whether it is sports, music or movies.

Karen: The entertainment value cannot be emphasized enough, but celebrities shouldn't be such a big deal so that we are totally obsessed with them.

SECTION B   PASSAGES

In this section, you will hear several passages. Listen to the passages carefully and then answer the questions that follow.

Questions 11 to 13 are based on the following passage. At the end of the passage, you will be given 15 seconds to answer the questions.

Now listen to the passage.

If you ask Americans why they intend to marry, most will tell you they marry for love. Committed to the idea that romantic love and marriage naturally go hand in hand, most Americans don't realize that not all societies share the belief that a marriage is based on romance. Korean dating services, for example, spend little time trying to match people on the basis of romantic attraction. What they do is bring together those with similar backgrounds and traditions.

Unaware of cultural differences, most Americans also don't know that throughout much of history, romantic love was simply not a requirement for marriage. For members of the upper classes, who had the time to think of such things, romantic love was usually pursued outside marriage. As one might expect, the poorer classes were too busy trying to stay alive to worry about romance. It is only in the last century or two, that the modern notion of love and marriage had firmly planted itself in the American mind. Rich or poor, almost everyone believed that romance was essential to marriage. In fact, in a 1986 study, the majority of college students surveyed insisted they would never marry someone they hadn't fallen deeply in love with, even if that person had every other quality they considered desirable in a mate.

Questions 14 to 17 are based on the following passage. At the end of the passage, you will be given 20 seconds to answer the questions.

Now listen to the passage.

Women are quite often competent drivers, but they are seldom first-class. At best they pose a mild danger, at worst they can be deadly. A wise male driver will always give women plenty of road and still be on the look-out for the unpredictable to happen. This deficiency has nothing to do with their lack of ability to cope with the mechanical complexities of the vehicle. It is due to an inherent characteristic which, in certain other circumstances, may be highly desirable, but which, behind the wheel, is deadly. This is their desire for talking. When women talk, simple words are not enough. They look into each other's faces to see the expression which accompanies the words and read the meaning that the words do not say. Thus two women in the front of a car repeatedly distract each other's attention from the road.

Quite apart from this factor, women seldom use the driving mirror except for cosmetic purposes, after which its position gives little indication of the state of the road behind.

A final important factor that seems to lie at he back of female attitudes toward driving is that relatively few women have the feel for a machine that so many men have; the satisfaction of a slick change of gear means nothing to them. The coordination of driving which gives men a boost of pride is only a temporary break in their concentration on the topic in hand.

Questions 18 *to* 20 *are based on the following passage. At the end of the passage, you will be given* 15 *seconds to answer the questions.*

Now listen to the passage.

In India, the practice of arranged marriages cuts across class lines, regional boundaries and language barriers. Marriage is treated as a union between two families rather than two individuals. In a family where several generations are living together, the bride is evaluated on her suitability as part of the entire family environment rather than only as a wife to her husband. Love is not viewed as an important element in mate selection nor is courtship thought to be necessary for testing the relationship. In fact, romantic love is regarded as an uncontrollable and explosive emotion which interferes with the use of reason and logic in decision making. Love is thought to be a disruptive element since it implies a change of loyalty from the family to another individual. Thus, mate selection by self-choice is seen as endangering the stability of the entire family since it could lead to the selection of a mate of unsuitable temperament or background.

In urban areas of India, newspaper ads have become a convenient and acceptable method of finding a suitable mate. These advertisements typically list the characteristics of the young men and women that are considered desirable. In the Indian culture, a male is highly valued for the social and economic status of his family, his educational level and potential earning power. Personal qualities such as appearance and personality are not considered very important. In women the following qualities are emphasized: moral character, beauty, ability to cook well and manage a home, and education.

SECTION C   NEWS BROADCAST

Question 21 *is based on the following news. At the end of the news item, you will be given* 5 *seconds to answer the questions.*
Now listen to the news.

The United Nations' World Food Program issued a stark warning that it ran out of food in North Korea. The organization says more than six million people, a quarter of the country's population, will go without normal rations until new supplies arrive in April. Until then food aid will only be given to the neediest one hundred thousand people, mostly pregnant women and children in hospitals and orphanages.

Questions 22 *and* 23 *are based on the following news. At the end of the news item, you will be given* 10 *seconds to answer the questions*
Now listen to the news.

The United Nations children's organization UNICEF(联合国儿童基金会)says campaigns for universal education have not benefited girls as much as boys. In its annual report, UNICEF says some one hundred twenty million children miss primary school every year, and most of them are girls. It says the worst affected countries are in Sub-Saharan Africa and in South and East Asia.

In the most recent past in the last ten years, impact of HIV/AIDS has made a reversal on the gains that have been made. So that some of the most prosperous and progressive countries, particularly in southern Africa who had great hope for making certain that all their kids are educated and all their girls are educated are now dealing with the impact of AIDS, impact of AIDS in terms of teachers, children orphaned by AIDS, girls pulled out of school to take care of their families.

Questions 24 *and* 25 *are based on the following news. At the end of the news item, you will be given* 10 *seconds to answer the question.*
Now listen to the news.

Wal-Mart plans to hire an extra 150,000 staff in China over the next five years. The US firm currently has 56 stores in China and plans to open a further 20 over the next year. It plans to establish a university degree to help new staff acquire skills in food preparation and finance. The world's largest retailers are all looking to expand in China. Of the foreign retailers operating in China, French firm Carrefour currently leads the way with 78 stores. However, British firm Tesco and Germany's Metro are among a number of other companies planning to increase their share of market in China.

Questions 26 to 27 are based on the following news. At the end of the news item, you will be given 10 seconds to answer the questions.

Now listen to the news.

Russia and China have signed an agreement to send large quantities of gas from fields in Siberia to China. Officials said the pipelines, which could begin supply within five years, would deliver up to 80 billion cubic meters of gas annually. The agreement came as part of economic agreements signed between the two sides during the visit to Beijing of Russian President Vladimir Putin. The two sides have signed 15 agreements to promote commercial co-operation, including four relating to the energy sector. But what China really wants is an oil pipeline from Siberia.

Questions 28 to 30 are based on the following news. At the end of the news item, you will be given 15 seconds to answer the questions.

Now listen to the news.

A United Nation's study says the economic benefits of ending child labor in poor countries would greatly exceed the costs involved. The study by the International Labor Organization estimates the net gains to the world economy from sending all child laborers to school would be more than four trillion dollars over a period of twenty years.

In what's said to be the first study of its type the International Labor Organization has investigated the cost of ending the social evil of child labor in poor nations. The research concludes the global bill for eliminating the practice would be some seven hundred and sixty billion dollars over a program lasting twenty years. That figure takes account of factors such as the costs of building new schools, employing more teachers, compensating poor families for the loss of their children's income and the loss of production to the wider economy. It may seem an enormous sum, but the ILO says it's far less than countries already spent on paying interest on debts.

TAPESCRIPT OF PRACTICE TEST 9

PART I DICTATION

Listen to the following passage. Altogether the passage will be read to you four times. During the first reading, which will be read at normal speed, listen and try to understand the meaning. For the second and third readings, the passage will be read sentence by sentence, or phrase by phrase, with intervals of 15 seconds. The last reading will be read at normal speed again and during this time you should check your work. You will then be given 2 minutes to check through your work once more.

Now listen to the passage.

GROWING COFFEE

Coffee is an important crop for the developing economies. / However, coffee growers are getting less for their crop/ even as the world market has grown. /

World coffee production has grown by about two-hundred percent since nineteen-fifty. / New growing methods have caused part of this increase. / Farmers have traditionally grown coffee under the cover of trees, often fruit trees. /

However, the introduction of chemical fertilizers and more productive kinds of coffee plants/ have changed the traditional methods. / Now, many coffee farmers grow their crop in full sun and use man-made fertilizers. /The result is a larger crop and too much coffee on the world market. /

The World Bank has suggested that farmers use traditional methods of growing coffee. / It has also studied production methods /

that permit better prices and continued development. /It calls this "sustainable coffee." /This kind of coffee requires more investment in coffee production methods. /

The second and third readings. You should begin writing now.

The last reading. Now, you have two minutes to check through your work.

PART Ⅱ   LISTENING COMPREHENSION

In sections A, B and C you will hear everything once only. Listen carefully and then answer the questions that follow.

SECTION A   CONVERSATIONS

In this section you will hear several conversations. Listen to the conversations carefully and then answer the questions that follow.

Questions 1 to 3 are based on the following conversation. At the end of the conversation, you will be given 15 seconds to answer the questions.

Now listen to the conversation.

Man: Honey, the football game is about to start. And could you bring some potato chips and a bowl of ice cream? And a slice of pizza from the fridge.

Woman: Anything else?

Man: Nope, that's all for now. Hey, honey, you know, they're organizing a school football team, and I'd like to join. What do you think?

Woman: Well, I don't know.

Man: I was the star player back in high school.

Woman: Yeah, that was thirty years ago. Look, I just don't want you to have a heart attack running around the court.

Man: So, what are you suggesting? You mean I should give up? But I'm still in good health.

Woman: Well, you should at least have a physical checkup before you begin. It has been, you know, at least five years since you played last time.

Man: Well, okay, but . . .

Woman: And you need to watch your diet and cut back on the fatty foods, like ice cream. And you should try eating more fresh fruits and vegetables.

Man: Yeah, you're probably right.

Woman: And you should take up a little weight training to strengthen your muscles or perhaps try cycling to build up your cardiovascular(心血管的)system. And you need to go to bed early instead of watching TV half the night.

Man: Hey, you're starting to sound like my personal fitness instructor!

Woman: No, I just love you, and I want you to be around for a long, long time.

Questions 4 *to* 7 *are based on the following conversation. At the end of the conversation, you will be given* 20 *seconds to answer the questions.*

Now listen to the conversation.

Emma: John, it's great you want to learn ballet.

John: But Emma, I'm 20 years old. Does that matter?

Emma: I myself danced as a child, but after a long break, I started dancing more seriously again at 19. It changed my body and attitude tremendously. Why do you want to learn ballet?

John: Well, I have the grace of an elephant and want to become fit. Although I don't plan on ever becoming a professional dancer, I would like to take it a little more seriously than just recreation. You know, I have the grace of an elephant and want to become fit.

Emma: I'm glad that you have realistic goals in your dance. I think it's wonderful to take dance seriously even if you don't have professional goals. It's a wonderful way to focus your energy into something that will develop you both mentally and physically. Taking it seriously will only increase the benefits.

John: I was wondering if you would be able to suggest any exercises that would help me with going on point. I was a hockey player in the past few years

Emma: Your strength as an athlete will certainly help you in your dancing, but you need to realize that you will be using your muscles very differently than in a hockey game.

John: Does ballet involve different muscles?

Emma: Ballet focuses on long, lean muscles rather than muscles that stand out so you will likely notice a change in the way your muscles look after you have been working for a while. If you are practicing your exercises correctly, you should notice that your muscles will lengthen.

Questions 8 to 10 are based on the following conversation. At the end of the conversation, you will be given 15 seconds to answer the questions.

Now listen to the conversation.

Jim: Laura, I'm falling in love.

Laura: Wow, congratulations!

Jim: You're an expert on love. Does falling in love simply mean feeling good about myself and my partner?

Laura: Well, there're a whole bunch of symptoms of falling in love: focused attention, excitement, heightened energy, obsessive thinking about the sweetheart and a desire for emotional union.

Jim: You said it. I don't feel like eating and sleeping. I'm deeply infatuated with her.

Laura: That's romantic love, which scientists say has neurological basis.

Jim: That's interesting.

Laura: Falling in love is an overwhelming experience. There's chemistry between you and your sweetheart, but the rush, that is, this sudden feeling of pleasure and excitement, will wear off over a period of time.

Jim: How come?

Laura: The chemicals that form the basis of romantic love last only a few years. After that couples are faced with the daunting task of keeping their relationship alive.

Jim: That's really disheartening.

Laura: What you need to do is treat your partner as a whole person, come to terms with the fact that nothing is perfect, be romantic like offering surprises, and communicate with your partner.

SECTION B   PASSAGES

In this section, you will hear several passages. Listen to the passages carefully and then answer the questions that follow.

Questions 11 to 13 are based on the following passage. At the

Poverty means different things to different people. That makes it difficult to determine how many people are poor in the world. The World Bank uses the so-called "dollar-a-day" standard. That means people living on less than a dollar a day are considered extremely poor. According to World Bank estimates, about 1. 3 billion people, or about one sixth of the world population, live in poverty today. Most are in developing countries.

But a manager in the World Bank's Development Research Group, says that despite the increase in Africa, global poverty has declined in the past twenty years. If you look at the developing world as a whole, things look pretty good. Over a 20-year period, the poverty rate has halved from about 40 percent to about 20 percent between 1981 and 2001.

But a Canadian professor thinks differently. The United States sets 14 dollars a day as a poverty level in the United States. We are living in the era of free trade, so for basic commodities such as food and fuel, the prices are not very different in developing countries. The cost of living in some of the developing countries is as high as in the United States. So people need to redefine poverty. If it takes two or three or four or five dollars a day to meet basic requirements, the levels of poverty in the world would be much, much higher.

Questions 14 *to* 17 *are based on the following passage. At the end of the passage, you will be given* 20 *seconds to answer the questions.*

Now listen to the passage.

Usually, the primary purpose of textbook writing is to inform. In textbooks, authors who are well-informed in a particular subject or discipline write about the terms and facts considered essential to an understanding of the field. While authors' personal interests play a role in what terms or facts are selected and how they are interpreted, the writing bears a primary or central goal which is not to persuade you to see things from the same perspective. In fact, textbook authors frequently give equal time to opposing points of views so that readers can draw their own conclusions.

However, as you turn from your textbook to the pages of newspapers and magazines, you may encounter writers with other primary goals. Some write to entertain; others write simply to express a personal preference. However, a good portion of the writers you encounter, particularly on the editorial pages, write in the hope that you will share or at least seriously consider adopting their opinion. They write, in short, with the desire to persuade. To achieve that goal, they may well give you an argument. That doesn't mean they force you or threaten you. It means they offer an conclusion—the opinion they want you to share—along with some reasons why you should share it. Critical readers try, first of all, to recognize those writers who wish to persuade. Then they analyze the arguments these writers provide.

Questions 18 *to* 20 *are based on the following passage. At the end of the passage, you will be given* 15 *seconds to answer the questions.*

Now listen to the passage.

Women, as a group, live longer than men. In all developed

countries and most undeveloped ones, women outlive men, sometimes by a margin of as much as 10 years. In the U. S. , life expectancy at birth is about 79 years for women and about 72 years for men. The gender difference is most pronounced in the very old: among centenarians worldwide, women outnumber men nine to one. The gender gap has widened in this century as gains in female life expectancy have exceeded those for males.

Although the reasons women live longer than men may change with time, it seems likely that women have been outliving men for centuries and perhaps longer. Even with the enormous risk caused by childbirth, women lived longer than men in 1900, and it appears that women have outsurvied men at least since the 1500s, when the first reliable mortality data were kept.

The fact that women live longer than men does not, however, mean that they necessarily enjoy better health. It could be that women live with their diseases, while men die from them. Indeed, there is a difference between the sexes in disease patterns, with women having more chronic nonfatal conditions—such as arthritis, osteoporosis(骨质疏松)and autoimmune(自身免疫的)disorders—and men having more fatal conditions, such as heart disease and cancer.

SECTION C　NEWS BROADCAST

Questions 21 *and* 22 *are based on the following news. At the end of the news item, you will be given* 10 *seconds to answer the questions.*

Now listen to the news.

The U. S. Labor Department says the number of Americans asking for unemployment compensation jumped by 30,000 last week, the biggest increase in over a year. The rise was larger than economists expected. Thursday's Labor Department's latest report says 360,000 people filed for unemployment compensation last week, compared to 330,000 the week before. The jump in unemployment claims is an exception to a series of reports pointing to a strengthening economy and an improving job market in the United States.

Questions 23 and 24 are based on the following news. At the end of the news item, you will be given 10 seconds to answer the questions.

Now listen to the news.

Doctors say Diego Maradona is responding to treatment for heart and blood pressure problems, two days after the Argentine football legend was admitted to the hospital. Maradona's long-time personal physician said Tuesday that the soccer star is still on a respirator in the intensive care unit, but that he has shown clear improvement. He said Maradona is still being closely monitored. He denied that cocain was the cause of the latest health problems.

Treatment for the controversial former player, who has battled drug addiction for years, has been complicated by an infection in both lungs, but he is expected to respond positively to antibiotics. His respirator is on a low setting and it could be removed as early as Wednesday if his condition continues improving.

Questions 25 and 26 ares based on the following news. At the end of the news item, you will be given 10 seconds to answer the question.

Now listen to the news.

Although the United States leads the world in medical technology, government health officials find that many Americans are no strangers to traditional medicine. According to a survey of 31,000 in 2002, 36 percent of them use herbal remedies, acupuncture, yoga, massage, special diets or some combination of these. Many Americans, 43 percent, also pray to achieve health benefits. In addition, deep breathing and meditation are also popular among about 10 percent of the people questioned.

The poll finds that people turn to such ancient techniques mostly to cure pain and colds, anxiety and depression, even though there may be a drug or other sophisticated medical therapy available to deal with the problem. It may be that the public is turning to complementary and alternative medicine because it's not getting relief from conventional medicine. The survey found that 28 percent of the people who responded to the survey said they used complementary and alternative medicine and did so because they thought conventional medicine would not help them.

Questions 27 and 28 are based on the following news. At the end of the news item, you will be given 10 seconds to answer the questions.

Now listen to the news.

A town in the U. S. state of Massachusetts says it has found a document suggesting baseball was played there more than 200 years ago.

Officials in Pittsfield say a reference to the sport was recently found in an 1869 book on the town's history. The book describes a law, passed in 1791, banning baseball from being played near Pittsfield's meeting house.

The long-accepted story of baseball's origins centers around Abner Doubleday, who is said to have written the first rules for the sport in 1839. The first real baseball game is believed to have been played in Hoboken, New Jersey in 1846.

Experts say it may be impossible to determine whether the baseball referred to in the Pittsfield law is the same sport known today. Modern baseball evolved from earlier sports, including the English games of cricket and rounders(跑柱式棒球).

Questions 29 and 30 are based on the following news. At the end of the news item, you will be given 10 seconds to answer the questions.

Now listen to the news.

A survey of more than 1,500 people conducted by market analysts Mintel found that 52 percent of British adults favor a ban on smoking in places like pubs and restaurants.

Sixty-seven percent of non-smokers were likely to support a ban, but even among smokers, almost three-in-ten also favored the proposal. However, 25 percent of smokers said they would avoid places where the ban was in force.

A research study published this week in Britain said that passive or second-hand smoking kills hundreds of Britons each year. Several medical institutions have urged the government to ban smoking in pubs, restaurants and workplaces.

The government has so far shown little interest in committing itself to such a ban. However, pressure is building for Britain to follow the lead of Ireland, which banned smoking in public places in March.

TAPESCRIPT OF PRACTICE TEST 10

PART Ⅰ DICTATION

Listen to the following passage. Altogether the passage will be read to you four times. During the first reading, which will be read at normal speed, listen and try to understand the meaning. For the second and third readings, the passage will be read sentence by sentence, or phrase by phrase, with intervals of 15 seconds. The last reading will be read at normal speed again and during this time you should check your work. You will then be given 2 minutes to check through your work once more.

Now listen to the passage.

THE UNITED NATIONS ON ROAD SAFETY

The United Nations has called for a campaign to improve road safety. / It is estimated that road traffic kills more than one-million people a year. / Road crashes are a leading cause of death among people age five to forty-four. /Road injuries cost one to two percent of national earnings in many less developed nations. /

In rich countries, the people most at risk of traffic injuries are drivers and passengers. /However, in poor nations, people walking or riding bicycles are among those at greatest risk. /So are those using public transportation. /

The U. N. calls for a government agency in each country/ to coordinate efforts to improve national road safety. /It also calls for stronger traffic laws and stronger enforcement. /

The U. N. urges more education about the need to use safety equipment like seatbelts. /And it calls for teaching more about the dangers of driving too fast/ and driving under the influence of alcohol or drugs. /

The U. N. warns about what could happen without immediate action. /It estimates that road traffic deaths in less developed countries will increase by eighty percent.

The second and third readings. You should begin writing now.

The last reading. Now, you have two minutes to check through your work.

PART II   LISTENING COMPREHENSION

In sections A, B and C you will hear everything once only. Listen carefully and then answer the questions that follow.

SECTION A   CONVERSATIONS

In this section you will hear several conversations. Listen to the conversations carefully and then answer the questions that follow.

Questions 1 to 3 are based on the following conversation. At the end of the conversation, you will be given 15 seconds to answer the questions.

Now listen to the conversation.

Rose: Alan, do you like watching television?

Alan: I used to watch an awful lot of television. In fact, I was quite addicted to it.

Rose: How much did you watch?

Alan: I watched 5 hours of television every night without including the weekends. I don't think you want to hear about the weekends.

Rose: Possibly not. When did you give it up?

188

Alan: Only a week ago. And one of the greatest lessons I have learned this past week is how to view time. I used to have "spare time" which I often looked at as "time to kill." But I realized that time is one of the most valuable commodities we have.

Rose: How do you spend your time now?

Alan: Instead of killing it, I now use it to do something worthwhile, such as the study of literature.

Rose: You've been without television for just a week. Do you think you can really give it up?

Alan: I think old habits do indeed die hard, and I don't think I'll be getting rid of my television completely just yet. But after my week-long experiment, I feel like I am back in the driver's seat. Now I realize that I have to control my television watching, and not let it control me.

Questions 4 *to* 7 *are based on the following conversation. At the end of the conversation, you will be given* 20 *seconds to answer the questions.*

Now listen to the conversation.

Wendy: Tracy, how do you pay for your collage education?

Tracy: Well, I am very lucky. My husband works full time, so with his salary and my student loan, we can just afford to own our own apartment near the college.

Wendy: So money is not an issue to you?

Tracy: Money is still the thing most likely to keep me awake at 4 a. m. How people survive on a student loan alone is beyond me.

Wendy: You're pretty independent, I mean you don't ask your

parents for money.

Tracy: The fact of matter is, my parents made too much money for me to qualify for any grants. Also, my parents had always spent every dime they made and, as a result, had not saved up anything for my college education

Wendy: Do you pay a lot for non-college expenses?

Tracy: I know I should cut corners. But sometimes I spend money on evening out with friends, road trips and vacations. I'm not the person who can say "no" easily.

Wendy: There are lots of experts out there telling students how to budget their money. Do you listen to their advice?

Tracy: What they say makes lots of sense to me, but for many people, it's one thing to get expert opinions and it's quite another to follow them through.

Questions 8 to 10 are based on the following conversation. At the end of the conversation, you will be given 15 seconds to answer the questions.

Now listen to the conversation.

Peter: Cathy, have you ever dated on the Internet?

Cathy: Yes. I met several men in chat rooms.

Peter: Did you meet someone face to face?

Cathy: Well, I did meet one man in person.

Peter: Wow. Can you tell me about it?

Cathy: Before we met, we chatted a lot on the Internet. And then I saw his photograph and I immediately liked the look of him.

Peter: What was it like when you actually met him, was he the man that you thought you knew via the Internet, or was this someone different, had he put on a mask at all?

190

Cathy: No, certainly there wasn't a mask and when we did meet, there was a bit of shock for me.

Peter: What was the shock?

Cathy: Before we met in person, I was so familiar with his persona (人物表象). And all of a sudden there was the physical representation of it, and, don't get me wrong, I wasn't put off in any way. Quite the contrary, because all of a sudden you saw the real person with your own eyes, and there was touching and hearing and getting used to somebody's voice and it was a totally different experience.

Peter: But many people in chat rooms are anonymous. They can wear any mask they want. So how often is it that you're likely to meet someone that is real?

Cathy: Well I think there are masks and there's a risk, but as long as you approach this cautiously I don't think that's too much a risk.

SECTION B   PASSAGES

In this section, you will hear several passages. Listen to the passages carefully and then answer the questions that follow.

Questions 11 to 13 are based on the following passage. At the end of the passage, you will be given 15 seconds to answer the questions.

Now listen to the passage.

What makes River Bend special is its community of neighborhoods that suit almost every lifestyle, income and family size. River Bend consists of individual neighborhoods, each containing approximately 20 to 30 homes. Large enough to allow for a neighborhood identity, yet small enough to develop a sense of

191

genuine friendliness.

For security and privacy, all residential streets are circles or short lanes, resulting in very little traffic. Beautiful gardens surrounding each home further increase the peaceful feeling of a small neighborhood. And whatever your preference for housing style and price, there is a River Bend neighborhood just for you.

In the first place, River Bend offers high-quality town homes and a wide variety of affordable single-family homes that make a very wise investment. Also are available at River Bend are large homes with plenty of space to suit your expanding needs in designs from traditional to rural.

In River Bend there is a community-wide system of sports facilities. There is a big swimming pool providing separate areas for swimming, diving and family fun. Six championship tennis courts provide the perfect conditions for players of all levels. The multipurpose athletic field is ideal for football, volleyball, or any other game you play.

Preserving the beauty of River Bend's natural surroundings are open spaces and greenways where residents can walk and relax. And all neighborhoods and facilities are joined by a network of footpaths that safely avoid traffic.

Questions 14 *to* 17 *are based on the following passage. At the end of the passage, you will be given* 20 *seconds to answer the questions.*

Now listen to the passage.

You're lost in a foreign city and don't speak the language and are late for the meeting. What do you do?

Take out your cell phone, photograph the nearest building and press SEND.

For a small fee, photo recognition software will figure out exactly where you are, and give you directions that will get you to your destination. At least, that is what some researchers at the University of Cambridge, UK, hope their software will one day do.

They have developed a program that can match a photo of a building to a database of images. The database contains a three-dimensional(三维立体的)model of the real-life street, so the software can tell where the user is, to within one meter.

This is far better than existing systems can manage. GPS (Global Positioning System) satellite positioning is accurate to 10 meters at best. And cell phone positioning has a range of between 50 and 100 meters.

The new software, on the other hand, can tell which direction you are facing. So the service can give a set of directions such as "turn to your left and start walking." The service can also give information on the building in the photograph.

The software can match two images even when they are taken at different times of day, from different angles and with pedestrians and vehicles in the way.

As to the system's commercial future, it's still unclear how much people are prepared to pay for it, and how often will they use it.

Questions 18 *to* 20 *are based on the following passage. At the end of the passage, you will be given* 15 *seconds to answer the questions.*

Now listen to the passage.

Bookworms are insects that feed on the covers and glue of books.

Human bookworms feed on words and ideas contained in books. Human bookworms probably got their not so attractive name because of the one quality they share with real bookworms, that is, they spend most of their time around books.

Most people think of bookworms as passive, dull, even lazy —a lot like real worms. The only reason they move is to turn a page. People who view bookworms as passive don't realize how rapidly bookworms' minds are moving and how far these "passive" people are traveling. Through their reading, bookworms encounter other cultures and get to understand controversial issues.

Reading is very much an individual hobby. Many non-readers believe that because bookworms spend so much time alone, they are disconnected and antisocial. Though bookworms may spend large amounts time glued to the pages of a book, they are connected to the universe in extremely responsible ways. Many bookworms use what they have learned from books to do a lot of good in the world.

Like the creatures they were named after, bookworms don't seem to lead very exciting lives. Don't be too hasty in judging bookworms by their appearance, though. For one thing, bookworms are usually interested in more than one subject and therefore are more interesting to talk to than someone who focuses on only one special interest.

SECTION C   NEWS BROADCAST

Questions 21 *and* 22 *are based on the following news. At the end of the news item, you will be given* 10 *seconds to answer the questions.*

Now listen to the news.

A new U. N. report says millions of lives could be saved in

coming decades if developing countries make better preparations to reduce the danger to their people from natural disasters. The United Nations Development Fund says much of the death and destruction caused by natural disasters in poor countries could be avoided by better planning.

The report by the U. N. Development Fund says death rates are much higher in poor countries than in rich nations, even though the frequency and intensity of disasters are the same. The co-author of the report, Andrew Maskrey, says that that does not have to be the case, and governments in developing countries can save thousands of lives if they make better development decisions. Mr. Maskrey says the impact of disasters could be cut sharply if more governments would make an effort to reduce the danger before a disaster happens.

Questions 23 *and* 24 *are based on the following news. At the end of the news item, you will be given* 10 *seconds to answer the questions.*

Now listen to the news.

Astronomers have found an enormous ball of ice and dust far beyond Pluto(冥王星). This minor planet is by far the most distant object ever seen in our solar system.

Last November, astronomers searched the sky for minor planets and got a glimpse of a new one. Over the past several months of study they've grown increasingly excited about what they found. The object turns out to be in an oblong（长椭圆形的）orbit that carries it up to a thousand times farther from the sun than the earth is. That makes it the most distant object in our solar system by far. Neptune (海王星), for comparison, is only 30 times farther from the sun than the earth is. Astronomers have named the object Sedna. They can't say for sure how big Sedna is, but their best guess right now is that it's about half the diameter of Pluto. That makes it one of the largest objects other than planets and moons found in our solar system.

Questions 25 and 26 are based on the following news. At the end of the news item, you will be given 10 seconds to answer the question.

Now listen to the news.

The US Senate has passed a landmark bill aimed at ending the country's budget deficits within the next seven years. It would cut government spending by more than 900,000 million dollars. Health, education and hundreds of other programs will be hit. The bill was passed last week by the House of Representatives. And congressional leaders now have to work out a compromise. A BBC Washington correspondent says the stage is now set for a confrontation with the White House. President Clinton has threatened to veto the Republican plans.

Questions 27 and 28 are based on the following news. At the end of the news item, you will be given 10 seconds to answer the questions.

Now listen to the news.

A team of surgeons in Dallas, Texas, has separated two-year-old conjoined twins(连体双胞胎) from Egypt after a 26-hour operation, and all appears to have gone well. The delicate and difficult procedure to separate the two twin brothers who were joined at the head began on Saturday and ended 26 hours later at midday Sunday Dallas time. The twin brothers are put in a coma while plastic surgeons continue

196

to work at reconstructing the skulls and closing the wounds at the top of each young patient's head. Doctors say the operation was possible because the two brains were almost completely separate, but that the cutting through the complicated blood vessels in their heads without causing permanent damage was a major challenge. If the two boys are awaken moving their arms and legs a week from now, it will be an indication that they have survived the procedure with minimal side effects.

Questions 29 and 30 are based on the following news. At the end of the news item, you will be given 10 seconds to answer the questions.

Now listen to the news.

The final of the African Cup of Nations will be contested by two North African teams, Morocco and Tunisia. Morocco overwhelmed Mali by four goals to nil(零). The host Tunisia beat Algeria five three in a penalty shootout(罚点球决胜负).

Algeria, Morocco and Egypt have all won this competition in the past and Tunisia feels left out, especially as the country has been to three World Cups and is also holding this event for the third time. For a nation that claims to be extremely patriotic it's ironic that they are being guided to the final by a French coach and assisted by two Brazilians who are naturalized(使加入国籍) after playing in the local league. In Saturday's final Tunisia will play against Morocco, the first time two North Africans have faced each other in twenty four of these finals.

第四部分　答案

PRACTICE TEST 1

1. B　2. A　3. B　4. A　5. C　6. B　7. D　8. B　9. C　10. B
11. A　12. D　13. B　14. D　15. B　16. C　17. C　18. D　19. D　20. C
21. C　22. B　23. A　24. D　25. B　26. A　27. B　28. A　29. A　30. B

PRACTICE TEST 2

1. A　2. B　3. C　4. D　5. D　6. C　7. A　8. A　9. D　10. D
11. B　12. B　13. D　14. D　15. C　16. D　17. C　18. B　19. B　20. C
21. B　22. D　23. B　24. C　25. A　26. A　27. A　28. B　29. B　30. C

PRACTICE TEST 3

1. D　2. A　3. A　4. C　5. C　6. D　7. A　8. C　9. B　10. A
11. A　12. D　13. C　14. B　15. D　16. A　17. B　18. D　19. C　20. D
21. C　22. C　23. A　24. A　25. C　26. C　27. C　28. A　29. D　30. A

PRACTICE TEST 4

1. A　2. D　3. A　4. B　5. A　6. B　7. A　8. B　9. C　10. C
11. D　12. D　13. C　14. D　15. B　16. A　17. A　18. B　19. C　20. D
21. A　22. A　23. A　24. A　25. B　26. A　27. C　28. A　29. C　30. D

PRACTICE TEST 5

1. C　2. C　3. D　4. A　5. D　6. D　7. C　8. C　9. C　10. A
11. C　12. A　13. B　14. D　15. A　16. B　17. D　18. A　19. D　20. D
21. B　22. B　23. D　24. A　25. B　26. D　27. B　28. D　29. C　30. D

PRACTICE TEST 6

1. C 2. D 3. A 4. B 5. D 6. B 7. C 8. B 9. C 10. A
11. B 12. A 13. B 14. A 15. A 16. D 17. C 18. C 19. B 20. C
21. C 22. C 23. B 24. D 25. B 26. A 27. A 28. D 29. D 30. B

PRACTICE TEST 7

1. C 2. C 3. C 4. B 5. C 6. D 7. B 8. D 9. B 10. D
11. A 12. C 13. B 14. A 15. C 16. D 17. D 18. B 19. C 20. D
21. C 22. A 23. C 24. D 25. B 26. C 27. B 28. D 29. B 30. C

PRACTICE TEST 8

1. B 2. A 3. A 4. D 5. B 6. A 7. B 8. C 9. C 10. C
11. A 12. C 13. A 14. B 15. D 16. C 17. C 18. A 19. D 20. A
21. D 22. C 23. C 24. C 25. B 26. C 27. A 28. C 29. C 30. D

PRACTICE TEST 9

1. C 2. D 3. A 4. C 5. A 6. A 7. B 8. D 9. A 10. A
11. C 12. B 13. C 14. B 15. D 16. C 17. C 18. B 19. C 20. B
21. D 22. B 23. C 24. C 25. D 26. A 27. D 28. B 29. A 30. A

PRACTICE TEST 10

1. C 2. C 3. C 4. C 5. D 6. C 7. D 8. D 9. A 10. D
11. B 12. B 13. B 14. D 15. B 16. D 17. D 18. B 19. B 20. C
21. D 22. C 23. A 24. A 25. C 26. B 27. D 28. C 29. C 30. C